Love Changes

Marsha Casper Cook

ISBN: 978-1-60414-1-948

Other books by Marsha Casper Cook

Grand Central

It's All About Love

Every Man Wants Her

It's Never Enough

Stepping Up Her Game

The Virginia Templeton Stories

To Life

It's Never Too Late

No Clues No Shoes

Snack Attack

The Busy Bus

Isabella Pimpinella's Magical Potion

Love Changes

Love changes as does life
Like the seasons come upon us
A gift may appear
We may not notice it at first
Maybe a few words are spoken
Maybe a whisper or a smile
Maybe a laugh or two
Something happens to make us wonder
Why we feel different
We feel alive
We smile
We whisper sweet words
We laugh
Something is different
We have changed
We feel wonderful
We feel special
We are alive
We have found the perfect gift

Acknowledgments

This book is dedicated to loving your children for who they are, and never forgetting that there is nothing greater than hearing the word, "Mommy."

To my son Marcus, thank you so much for enjoying this story enough to say, "Go for it."

To my husband Stephen, thank you so much for letting me be who I am, and for never complaining about how much time I spend working.

I would like to thank my family and friends for supporting me once again in my efforts to make dreams become realities.

I would also like to give special thanks to my editor Jeff Fleischer, who has most definitely been the driving force in helping me get this novel ready for print.

And, last but not least, to Bonnie and Pat, two great friends who listen to and read every project I work on.

Chapter 1

It was time. The music had stopped. As a well-dressed man slowly walked to the podium, the crowd was appropriately quiet. Faint sounds were heard as the waiters filled the goblets with champagne for the toast.

"Good evening to all our guests from Chicago, and those of you not from Chicago, we welcome you. I am Cecil Aronson, and who better than I to present tonight's award to my colleague and lifelong friend, Dr. Martin Lewis. The man with a vision, the man with a heart of gold."

Cecil briefly stopped his speech as the audience applauded. The spotlight transferred away from Cecil to shine on Martin. As always, Martin's smile was contagious. He stood up as the crowd applauded.

Recognizing it was not quite time to join his friend Cecil at the podium, Martin remained seated between his wife Elaine and his mother Esther.

Cecil continued his speech. "Martin and I go as far back as I can remember, third grade to be exact. Even at such a young age, Martin was every bit as conscientious as he is today. When something needed to be done, Martin went out and did it, and he did it well. No questions asked. For a man like Martin, there can be no other way. Even at such a young age, I was able to distinguish how lucky I was to have Martin as a friend, as we all are. He's a great guy to have in your corner. Not only does he succeed in his endeavors, he brings a great sense of pride and integrity to his projects. Thank goodness he chose the Meridian Hospital."

As Cecil spoke, Martin listened carefully to each and every word. However, Martin began to show visible signs of embarrassment. As his face turned red, he was thankful the spotlight had left his table and was once again centered on Cecil who, unlike Martin, loved notoriety.

Over the years, Martin had always kept his charitable donations anonymous, but this time the publicity surrounding the Rehabilitation Center couldn't be disguised.

He was the celebrity behind the scenes, but after tonight it would be over. He would go back to his practice. Delivering babies was far too rewarding for Martin to imagine himself doing anything else.

To Martin, each new life he helped bring into the world was very special. In fact, his greatest possession was the photo collection of all the babies he had delivered.

Cecil stopped for a brief moment to once again wait for the spotlight to shift toward Martin's table. Cecil continued on with what was turning into quite a lengthy speech, one which he no intention of making, but the excitement of the evening had changed everything. And who better than Cecil to spontaneously talk?

Cecil's speech was a tribute to a man who truly deserved praise and anything that went with it. If that meant a lengthy speech and respective applauding, so be it.

Martin looked at Cecil, trying to catch his eye. Cecil did notice Martin's uneasiness, but that didn't stop him. He was intent on really getting to the heart and soul of the night. Martin deserved every bit of the honor, and Cecil was there to make sure it happened.

"Three years ago, the Rehabilitation Center for the Development of Emotionally and Physically Handicapped Persons was a mere vision. Martin Lewis took that vision and made it reality. So, my friend, please come up and join me as I present you with this award for the most deserving of all doctors. You are the first director of the Meridian Rehabilitation Center, and we thank you for all the tireless hours, efficient planning and everything else it took to make the center possible. It's the best in the country and we can thank you for that."

Martin walked to the stage with all the excitement and enthusiasm of a man with great devotion. As Cecil handed Martin the magnificent, solid-gold plaque, Martin gave his friend a tight bear hug, reminding him of all they had gone through to get to the place they now stood.

Martin smiled at all the well-wishers, then focused his eyes toward his wife. "I think I shall begin with a heartfelt thank you to my family and friends. I was, or should I say I am, quite embarrassed by my good friend Cecil's words. I couldn't help but feel 'why me?' I have really only done what had to be done. Sometimes life isn't very fair. I suppose somewhere along the line, we'll all learn the reason why some are born into this world with just one too many problems. We may even find out just why in the prime of a person's life, they find themselves needing assistance in everything they do.

"That is why we are here. To learn and to love. So to those of our patients who try their hardest to complete their everyday tasks, I say keep trying, because you will do it. I know you will but, first and foremost, I want you to believe you will. For those of you who have joined us tonight and have disabilities, I will not ask you to stand, but I will ask you to listen to what your heart is saying. I stand here as a man who has lost and come back a winner, so I know it can be done. I will help you, as will the others here tonight. Some of the men and women you see here tonight will not be there for you on a daily basis but they are here for you, as they have shown with their generous donations. These are the people who have raised the necessary funds to get the job done, which we did. I stand here now and accept this award for everyone in this room because the Meridian Rehabilitation Center is a piece of all of us here tonight. Thank you, my friends."

Elaine watched as her husband once again won over the crowd with his kind words. He was a good man, a far better man than she had ever deserved. She knew she should love him more, but she couldn't.

Martin reached over to one of the head waiters for a glass of champagne. Lifting his glass toward the microphone, he spoke with the greatest of pleasure, "Please join me in a toast. To a world without pain and sadness. To a world where everyone walks with dignity and a sense of well-being. To life and the best if can be."

Esther Lewis applauded her son as he walked back to the table. "I'm a lucky woman," she said with a smile that wouldn't quit.

Martin seemed surprised. "I've never heard you say that before."

Esther didn't respond at first, then she said, "Well, I should have. Believe me, I'm sorry I didn't. Your father, may he rest in peace, always felt that way. He said it often, but I didn't. Is it too late?"

Martin kissed his mother's cheek and answered with complete honesty. "It's never too late, but I'll let you in on a secret. I always knew you felt that way."

Esther reached for her daughter-in-law's hand and squeezed tightly. "Elaine, my dear, we're two very lucky women."

Elaine smiled politely in response.

Chapter 2

It was six in the morning. Martin was just about to leave their bedroom when Elaine sat up in bed, rubbed her overtired eyes and called out, "Don't forget the symphony tonight!"

Martin walked back toward Elaine and sat down on the edge of their bed. "Good morning," he said, not expecting an answer just yet. It usually took Elaine a couple of minutes to accustom herself to early mornings.

"I didn't have the heart to wake you. Seems like you barely got any sleep last night .You tossed for the better half of the night," he added.

"I'm sorry if I kept you up," she apologized.

"You didn't. I keep myself up. That's when I do my planning. It's those wee hours in the morning when there's complete quiet and the only sounds you can hear are the birds chirping on the windowsill. That's when everything becomes clear and fresh. It's always been that way for me. It works."

"You won't forget the symphony, will you?" she reminded him.

Martin smiled. "Have I ever?"

"No, but you might."

"Not on your life. You know I don't like the symphony, but it's the only place I see you smile. For that alone, I'll be there."

Elaine rested her arm on Martin's knee. "You're such a good man."

"That's what they tell me," Martin jokingly boasted. "But I like it best when you tell me. The words seem to have a much greater impact."

After getting up from the bed, Martin kissed Elaine, not knowing what her reaction would be. It differed depending on the day.

On that day, Elaine hugged Martin tighter than usual. She hadn't intended to cry, but she did. Martin had become accustomed to her sudden, teary outbreaks. He never really understood why she had them so often. Ironically, neither did she.

"Elaine, are you alright?" Martin asked with his usual, concerned interest.

"Yes, I'm okay. Go ahead to work. I'll be fine. See you tonight."

Martin reluctantly left, realizing if Elaine's behavior didn't change soon, he would have to suggest she see a doctor. That was not something he looked forward to. He was certain she would fight him tooth and nail on that issue, as she had done in the past.

*****

It was early afternoon when Elaine arrived at Arlington Racetrack. The elevator to the clubhouse was exceptionally crowded for a weekday, but to Elaine it didn't make much difference. She had reserved the same table for the entire summer. Money was of no concern to her. If it took an extra twenty, fifty or sometimes a crisp, hundred-dollar bill to help matters along, so be it.

Having money did help with life's daily struggles. But long range, money could do nothing to change her sadness. Unhappiness was a permanent way of life for Elaine.

Elaine hadn't been seated for more than a minute or so when a waiter approached her table. He placed a large pitcher of lemon water and a basket of rolls on the stark, white tablecloth.

Elaine smiled, appreciative of the young waiter's acute sense of recall. They didn't speak much, but he smiled when she did.

As always, Elaine had not placed a bet on the first or second race. That was her time for gatherings thoughts and pulling the loose ends of the day together.

Some days she placed bets on only a few races. Those were the days when her mind wandered, remembering what she was trying so hard to forget. It was on those days that she usually picked the winners. But of course, she didn't care. That really wasn't why she came.

The ten-minute bell rang. It was the third race. Elaine reached inside her bag and pulled out several hundred-dollar bills. She crumpled them as she walked toward the betting counter. With a brief glance, she pointed to a number and handed the money to the woman at the window.

The race ended. Elaine had won. She paid little attention to the fact that she had bet on a winner.

A bolt of lightning flashed. Seconds later, a voice over the loudspeaker called out, "Due to severe weather, we are canceling the remainder of today's races."

Disappointed voices filled the clubhouse. Just as everyone seemed to be leaving, Elaine felt a tap on her shoulder. She looked up, not recognizing the young man who stood before her.

"Hello," he said in a very mellow voice.

"Do I know you?" Elaine asked in a swift, uninterested voice.

The young man's smile was attentive. "Yes, as a matter of fact you do. We met at an art showing. You were with Sally Braverman. Now do you remember?"

"No, I'm sorry I don't."

"That's okay. It was only my art showing and my art gallery. I guess it was foolish of me to think you might remember."

A brief but apologetic smile appeared on Elaine's face. "Oh yes, now I remember."

"Thank goodness," he laughed. "I thought I was losing my touch. Although, you might be good for my ego. You know, the ego I just lost."

They shared a smile.

Holding out his hand, the young man introduced himself. "I'd better not embarrass myself any more by thinking you know my name, so I'll make it easy on myself. Josh Derman."

Elaine was just about to say her name when Josh interrupted. "Elaine Lewis. Am I right?"

Elaine nodded, surprised by his memory.

Josh was just about ready to sit down when Elaine stood up. "You'll have to excuse me, but I should be leaving."

"Then I'll see you tomorrow," he said.

"I don't think so," Elaine responded quickly.

"You're here every day, so why not tomorrow?"

Elaine felt uneasy. "How do you know that?"

"Because I've seen you here every day for the last few weeks," Josh smiled.

Elaine didn't know what to say, so she didn't respond. Instead, she pleasantly smiled and walked away.

Josh didn't try to stop her as she walked toward the elevator. He just watched her leave, wishing they had been leaving together.

As Elaine drove home, she wondered why such an attractive man, obviously several years her junior, would be interested in her. She should have been flattered, but she was just curious.

***

It was almost five when Martin looked down at his watch. Realizing he might be late for the symphony, he telephoned Elaine. When there was no answer, he intertwined his hand with his son Stevie's and gave a tight squeeze. "What do you say we have some ice cream?" Martin asked, certain of the reply.

Excited by his father's idea, Stevie jumped up and gave Martin a big hug. For Martin, that was always the best part of their visit.

"Ice cream, Daddy! Ice cream!" Stevie shouted.

"Okay," Martin said. "All you have to do is hold onto my hand and we're off."

Stevie did just that, and they ran across the park, trying to catch the ice cream man before he gave his last clang.

Martin was slightly out of breath when he called out, "Wally, wait for us. Wally, we're on our way."

Just as Wally was about to get into his truck, he heard Martin. Wally yelled back, "It's okay Dr. Lewis. I'll wait for you and your little friend."

Martin tried to take a deep breath, but it was difficult. He ran too fast, but that was what he had to do to keep up with Stevie. As they approached the ice cream truck, Martin smiled, grateful that Wally had heard him.

Wally had been banging and clanging those chimes on the Good Humor truck for about as many years as Martin had been delivering babies. In fact, Martin had delivered Wally's four children, making them a bit more than friends.

With the help of a nitroglycerin pill, it only took a few seconds for Martin to feel better. Running wasn't the ideal sport for Martin, but when it came to ice cream, Stevie's excitement was all that mattered. As a matter of fact, Martin rarely thought about having Angina. That was how he dealt with the diagnosis. He knew he had it, but refused to allow it to change his life.

The truth was Martin would do just about anything to make Stevie happy. Stevie was the love of Martin's life, and he had never regretted Stevie's birth. Handicaps were just a label, nothing more. The only thing that mattered to Martin was love.

Being born a Down Syndrome child did not make Stevie different. It made him that much more special. However, the task of Elaine accepting Stevie still remained the dominant issue in their lives. Six years later, nothing had changed about Elaine's denial of being Stevie's mother.

Wally walked to the back of the truck and opened up the freezer compartment. "Chocolate cone today?" he asked.

A broad smile appeared on Stevie's face. "Yes … yes."

Wally noticed Martin was out of breath. "Are you okay, Doc?" he asked with concern.

As usual, Martin made light of his condition. "I'm fine, Wally. Don't worry about me. You know doctors, we never get sick. Anyway, enough about me. How're all my kids?"

"They're good. A bit mischievous, but luckily they haven't broken any walls lately. Kids do things like that, don't they?"

Martin gave Stevie a proud shoulder hug. "Yes they do. Oh well, thanks for waiting, Wally. See you soon," Martin added as he and Stevie walked toward the car.

***

Martin did arrive at the symphony on time. Elaine didn't ask Martin where he had been because she already knew. His daily visits to Stevie were acknowledged but never mentioned.

The orchestra had begun to play. Elaine's eyes were affixed toward center stage. She could feel her body loosen and her mind clear. Her only thought was on the magnificence of the music. Elaine's eyes closed as soon as she felt the splendor and harmony of the music consume her. She was at peace with herself, but it was only temporary. The only permanency left in her life was her disappointment.

Several times before intermission, Martin glanced down at his watch. Time seemed to be standing still. Finally, when his patience went out the door, he decided he would do the same. He nudged Elaine's shoulder. Elaine ignored Martin's first and second nudge, but by the fourth shoulder tap, Elaine couldn't very well overlook the issue anymore.

Elaine mouthed her anxiety. "Is something wrong?"

Martin answered quickly. "I have to call my service. I'll be right back."

Elaine looked directly into Martin's eyes and whispered in his ear. "I thought you weren't on call this evening."

A childlike expression appeared on Martin's face as he spoke a little louder than he should have. "You're right, you're absolutely right, I forgot."

A woman seated behind Martin poked her long, manicured fingernail into Martin's shoulder blade. "Be quiet. This is one of the very best parts," she said as she sat back in her seat and crossed her hands over her plentiful chest.

Martin turned to the woman and shook his head. "Sorry."

"Well, you should be," she more than whispered back.

Several minutes later, Martin whispered to Elaine, "Mind if I take a break?"

"No, go ahead."

Martin kissed Elaine's cheek as he hunched over and moved toward the aisle. He stepped over the man seated beside him, almost falling in his lap. Several people turned his way, watching Martin make an exit. By the look on some of the others' faces, he knew he wasn't the only one wanting to leave. But he was seemingly the only one with the nerve to make such an exit.

When he finally got into the lobby, he couldn't imagine himself going back in. So he didn't. He walked outside for a while and, when he lost interest in that, he came back inside, only to once again find himself not knowing what the hell to do.

At intermission, Elaine entered the lobby, trying to push her way through the crowds to find Martin. As much as she loved the symphony, she still hated running into people they knew.

It took less than a minute. There it was, that horrible tap on the shoulder. A fashionably dressed woman, exclusively Chanel, smiled and said, "Hello, my dear. How is that wonderful husband of yours?"

Elaine had no clue who this woman was, but she still replied politely. "He's fine, thank you."

Not wanting to be rude, she excused herself in a very ladylike manner. "If you don't mind, I must find Martin."

"Of course, by all means, dear. Say hello for me."

Elaine nodded as she rapidly walked toward the ladies' room. Luckily, she was stopped short by Martin.

"Martin, where have you been?"

He didn't answer. Instead, he placed his arm around her waist and walked her toward the door. "How about leaving early tonight? I've made reservations at Angelo's."

Elaine thought for a moment. "Okay, let's go."

Martin was stunned. "You're kidding, aren't you?"

"No, it's okay. You've been such a good sport. I know how you hate being here and anyway, I'm a little tired."

Getting over the shock, Martin turned to his wife and asked with sincerity, "Are you sure? We've never left this early. We can stay. I'll even go back in if you want to."

The moment Elaine walked out the door, Martin knew she was dead serious. It would have been ludicrous of him to stop her, so he didn't. Selfishly, he was happy.

Chapter 3

From the moment Martin and Elaine walked into Angelo's, they were treated as if they were family. That's how Angelo was, especially to Martin. Martin and his first wife, Iris, were Angelo's first paying customers. As far as Angelo was concerned, there would always be a soft spot in his heart for Iris Lewis. Her death hadn't changed a thing.

Angelo held out his hand to Martin. "Hello, Dr. Lewis. It's been quite a while. We've missed you. Saturday nights certainly aren't the same without you."

"We've tried, but it's been very hectic at the hospital. Now that things are quieting down, I think you'll be seeing more of us," Martin explained. "I've been imagining myself eating pasta primavera all day."

Angelo smiled, "I'm glad." Then, so as not to forget Elaine, Angelo reached for her hand. "And how are you, Mrs. Lewis?"

Elaine was brief. "I'm fine, thank you." She had always been aware of Angelo's feelings and decided against trying to win over his friendship. It wasn't going to happen.

Martin and Elaine followed Angelo as he escorted them to a very private table. "Tonight you are my guests. Whatever you want, it's yours," Angelo said with pride.

Martin smiled, reminding himself of all the times before. "It's not necessary."

"Yes it is," Angelo added with utmost sincerity.

That evening, Martin paid special attention to his wife's many distractions. Even before they ordered, Elaine nervously played with the silverware. First the knife, then the fork. Just as she was about to pick up her spoon, Martin reached across the table and took hold of her unsteady hands. "Now isn't that better? Are you sure you're alright?"

Elaine, somewhat on the defensive, answered, "I'm fine. Why?"

"To start with, you left the symphony early."

"What's so unusual about that?"

Before answering, Martin thought for a moment, trying not to upset Elaine with an answer that would cause her to become even more agitated than she had already been. "Correct me if I'm wrong, but we've been going to the symphony once a month for as long as we've been married."

Elaine nodded in agreement.

"Have we ever left early? God knows I've wanted to, but we never did. So why tonight?"

"I told you why. It's because you've been so good about taking me even though I know you would rather be doing just about anything else than listening to the symphony orchestra."

Martin was skeptical, but he continued. "And that's the only reason?"

"Yes. That's the only reason."

Martin went along with her, but he knew better. Something was wrong and, as usual, he didn't have a clue as to what it could be. Martin eased back against his chair, hoping the rest of the evening would improve.

During dinner, Martin initiated most of the conversation - in fact, Elaine barely spoke. Martin was certain she didn't hear a word he said, but the situation he faced was quite a familiar one.

Then, without thinking about the consequences or the right moment, Martin blurted out, "Okay, isn't it time you tell me what's on your mind?"

"Well," Elaine paused for a moment. "It's really not me this time. Just as you think you know me, I know you. You've spent the better half of the evening making small talk because you have something on your mind and you don't know how to weave it into the conversation."

A brief smile appeared on Martin's face. "I didn't think it showed."

"You never do," Elaine interrupted.

"Am I really that obvious?"

Elaine nodded. "Yes, always."

Martin took a long, deep breath before beginning. "I didn't schedule any patients today because I had so much paperwork, but a young woman came into the office. She didn't have an appointment but she looked desperate, so what else could I do but examine her?"

Suddenly, Elaine became very agitated and systematically stirred her spoon. Every third stir, she tapped the spoon twice. "Go on Martin, even though I know where this conversation is going," she added with an icy tone in her voice.

Martin stopped. He couldn't go on. Observing Elaine's behavior, he knew the outcome.

Elaine's eyes widened. "Martin, go on."

"I don't think so. We'll talk about this later."

"No, Martin go ahead. I want to hear the rest."

Against his better judgment, Martin bravely continued. "She's pregnant, not married and doesn't want to keep the baby. I thought, maybe..."

"Martin, you don't have to go any further. You thought you would talk to me and we could adopt her baby and the baby... we could give the baby a good home. That was what you were thinking, wasn't it?"

Martin's brief but comforting smile disappeared when he sensed the anxiety and tension that Elaine began to exhibit.

Elaine threw the napkin she had been twirling down on the table. "Martin, we agreed, no children."

In a softer voice than Elaine's, Martin pleaded. "I know we agreed no more children, but I think this might be the right avenue to take. I think a child would be good for us."

"For us? Or don't you really mean me?" Elaine demanded to know.

"I just thought ..."

Elaine quickly interrupted. "I know exactly what you thought. You thought if we had a child living in our home then, and I mean only then, would it be possible for you to blend someone else into our once-again-happy home."

Martin tried to calmly intercede. "Please Elaine, you can say his name. He's our son."

"That's where you're wrong. I don't have a son."

"Yes, you do. Stevie is our son."

Elaine stood up. She was just about ready to leave when Martin reached to grab her hand. "Please don't go. We won't talk about this anymore. The subject is closed," Martin promised in defeat.

"Alright, I'll be right back," Elaine reluctantly agreed. She then walked straight back toward the ladies' room and locked the door behind her. She leaned against the door and took several long, deep breaths. Sometimes that helped. When that didn't work, she walked over toward the sink and splashed her face with cold water. Several minutes had gone by before she felt somewhat composed. When she walked back to the table, her decision had been made. "Martin, I want to go home now," she pleaded.

By this time, Martin knew he had no choice. "Okay, why don't you wait for me by the door."

"Fine," Elaine said with relief in her voice.

Before leaving, Martin needed a moment alone. He sat at his table studying the room, admiring the other couples. Even without hearing their conversations, Martin envied their serenity.

As Martin stood up, Angelo came up from behind him. "I saw Mrs. Lewis leaving. Is everything alright?"

Martin was about to invent a lie, but when he saw the concern in Angelo's eyes, he told him the truth. "Elaine isn't feeling very well tonight."

Angelo seemed disappointed, but understood. "I'm so sorry this happened again."

As Martin shook Angelo's hand goodbye he added, with a great deal of sincerity, "Me too." Then he left.

***

In the privacy of their bedroom, Martin tried to comfort Elaine. Making love to her hadn't been as romantic as it had been when they first met. In fact, sometimes Martin felt as if she wasn't really there.

Many nights, Martin put the blame on himself. He would make excuses as to why it all seemed so different. He wanted to discuss their problems, but every time he even got close to the subject, Elaine either fell asleep or left the room.

Elaine was often very distant and, even when they kissed, Martin felt unsure of her love. Elaine, on the other hand, didn't concern herself with Martin's commitment. His love was always visible.

Tragically enough, Elaine wouldn't allow herself the luxury of wonderful lovemaking. From the very moment Stevie was born, she refused all chances to have even the smallest of pleasures come her way.

That night, after they had made love, Martin sat on the edge of their bed for a very long time. He watched Elaine sleep, reminding himself that they did have some very good times together. Of course, that was a long time ago.

Maybe it was presumptuous of him to want to feel close to his wife and share everything with her, but he knew that was never going to be possible.

He thought they had a good start, but it really wasn't the start that was important, it was how they would end up. He loved Elaine more than he imagined he ever could. But he knew his love wasn't ever going to be enough.

Martin deliberately closed his eyes and tried to fall asleep, but he couldn't. After a while, he quietly tiptoed toward the door, looking back at Elaine as he left. He felt content that she had finally fallen off to what appeared to be a calming sleep. He left their room hopeful that she would not be awoken by the horrible nightmares that besieged her.

As Martin approached the kitchen, he noticed the light was on. There sat Maggie. She was reading the paper and seemingly enjoying the milk and cookies she was munching on.

She hadn't noticed Martin enter the room until he sat down next to her. For years, Maggie had not only been Martin's housekeeper, but his confidant and maybe even his best friend.

Maggie was older and wiser and, although their heritage differed, her advice was always invaluable. There were times when without her help, Martin would have shattered and been unable to go on.

Maggie took off her reading glasses. "Can't sleep?"

"No," Martin said, pouring himself a glass of milk and nibbling on a chocolate-chip cookie.

"How's Mrs. Lewis?"

"Not very good. I don't know what to do. It's like she's self-destructing right before my very eyes. No matter what I do, I can't help her. The harder I try, the further away I get."

Maggie got up from the table, walked around to the back of Martin's chair and massaged his shoulders. "How long have we known each other?" she asked.

"I can't remember when we didn't."

"Well, then I guess you'll understand what I'm about to say to you. Your wife's in trouble. Real trouble."

Martin's face saddened with concern. "How do you know? Has Elaine said anything to you?"

"No, she doesn't have to. We're both women and I can see she's in a whole lot of pain."

Martin turned to Maggie and asked with real trepidation, "What should I do? I should have insisted she get help years ago, but I was afraid to. When Stevie was born, that was the time to confront the issue, but I did what she asked. I couldn't help myself, even though I knew it was a horrible thing to do. I loved her so, and I went along with her. Agreeing to tell my mother, my family and all our friends that Stevie was dead. What in the hell was I thinking? I don't think I did anybody a favor. But now, years later, I'm still afraid to push too hard."

"I know hon, you're afraid she'll leave," Maggie responded with her usual, recognizable compassion.

"You're right. I just couldn't bear it."

"There's an old saying, when true love exists it will survive any test you put it through," Maggie said, trying her best to reassure him. "Listen to what you're feeling inside and try to work from there."

A look of relief appeared on Martin's face. "When did you get to be so smart?"

"I'm not so smart. I'm just a woman who has loved. That's all."

***

Elaine's dream took her back six years, to a time when she was elated with the anticipation of her unborn child. When the most important concern in her life was the child she was carrying and the excitement of motherhood.

It was New Year's Eve, minutes away from a brand new year. Martin and Elaine had accepted their obligatory invitation to the annual New Year's Eve hospital party.

They usually brought in the new year alone, with a quiet dinner and a lovely bottle of champagne. But with a little extra coaxing from the committee chairman, none other than Cecil Aronson, they agreed to attend that year.

Just as the music stopped playing and the drum roll began, Elaine felt a sharp pain. After several more piercing jolts, she knew her labor had started. Elaine tapped Martin's shoulder and pointed to her stomach. "It's time to go," she said as she gently took hold of Martin's sleeve and tugged him toward the door.

The excitement on Martin's face was notable. He looked like the kid down the street who had just eaten the finest ice cream sundae ever made, the kind with lots of whipped cream and chocolate syrup.

Motioning to Cecil, he mouthed the words, "It's time to go. Baby time."

Cecil nodded as he also left the party.

Getting Elaine to the delivery room was quite an ordeal. Delivering babies was Martin's claim to fame, but on that night the tables had been turned. He was the father to be.

As unbelievable as it seemed, Martin missed the hospital entrance and found himself circling around the block. He had always joked about finding the maternity entrance blindfolded. But not that night.

His anxiety and loss of memory were corrected immediately, as Elaine bellowed out several loud cries of pain. He pulled up to the entrance, helped Elaine out of the car and wheeled her into maternity, at the same time forgetting he had left the keys in the car.

Martin wiped Elaine's brow as she nervously anticipated her delivery. He had also worked up quite a sweat. When Cecil Aronson saw how nervous Martin was, he couldn't help but find it amusing. "Okay, my friend, I think I had better take over now. Anyway, I think it might be a good idea if you parked your car in a space," Cecil said as he dangled the keys to Martin's car in front of his eyes.

Had anyone else noticed his slip-up, Martin would have been completely embarrassed. But Cecil understood, or at least pretended to.

Martin made light of his mistake as he reached for his keys and said, "You're right. Time to move that car of mine." He bent down and kissed Elaine's cheek. "Now don't you go anywhere."

Elaine gave him an odd look. "And where would I go? I think it's safe for you to assume that when you get back, I'll be here."

Cecil interrupted. "If we're not here when you return, you know where to find us."

When Martin returned, Elaine had already been prepped and was in a delivery room. Martin raced down the hall and quickly put on a gown, delighted he hadn't missed a thing. First babies usually took their time coming out.

Elaine smiled in relief when she noticed Martin standing beside her. She was slightly giddy, but very aware of this very special time. Martin grasped hold of her hand, not wanting to let go. Cecil looked at both of them and asked, "Elaine, are you ready?"

She nodded.

"And Martin, how about you? Shall we give it a go?"

Martin's face was glowing as he answered. "You bet."

After six very intense pushes, Elaine gave out a scream. She and her baby were ready. After one last push, Cecil looked at Martin. "Okay pal, here he comes..."

From that moment on, everything went wrong. Elaine's blood pressure dropped drastically and she began to bleed heavily. Cecil and his team of nurses and doctors looked at each other, recognizing trouble was upon them.

There was no more laughter or amusing jokes, just doctors and nurses doing their job. Whispers invaded the delivery room. Now it wasn't speculation, but fact. A serious problem had occurred and the staff did exactly what it had been trained to do.

Martin's eyes filled with tears as he looked at his son. He now knew something was very wrong.

At that point, Cecil surrendered the situation to the anesthesiologist.

It was all happening fast. Cecil took hold of Elaine's hand. "We're going to have to put you out now. But you're going to be just fine."

At that moment Elaine knew something horrible had happened. Elaine gave out a blood-curdling cry. "Oh no. My baby! Please God, no!"

***

The problems Elaine had acquired during delivery were repaired. Her loss of blood was not as severe as Cecil had expected, and her recuperation had already begun.

However, the most important problem could not be rectified. Elaine had delivered a son who had been born with Down Syndrome and without a name.

Martin, who stood there helpless during the delivery, wished he had not been there. This, his regular workplace, had now become uncomfortable for him. He had delivered hundreds of babies in that very same delivery room. But it wasn't until that night that he realized just how horrible it was to have a child born with a handicap.

God had made his decision and so did Martin. He would have his son circumcised and named. Steven Lewis might be handicapped, but he would be loved just the same.

The prognosis for Elaine's physical recovery was excellent, but her psychological pain couldn't be measured by time. Part of the reason plans couldn't be formulated was because Elaine had taken a stand. She insisted on no visitors, including Martin.

Three days had passed and Elaine still would not speak. Even during Cecil's examinations, Elaine never spoke. But she did stare at Cecil, hoping he would cut his visit short. It worked.

As her doctor and friend, Cecil tried to convince Elaine to see Martin. "Elaine, I know you're in pain, but so is Martin. He needs you and, whether you think so or not, you need each other."

Elaine didn't respond.

On the fifth day, Martin refused to observe Elaine's decision. He was determined to see his wife. It was noon, and lunch was about to be served. Elaine had not eaten anything in days, which concerned Martin.

As of that day, Cecil instructed the nurses to insist Elaine start eating on her own. They were to stay right at her side, to weigh and watch what she ate.

Martin cautiously opened the door with Elaine's lunch tray. She didn't say a word. Martin placed the tray on the table beside her and sat down. He held her hand for several minutes before speaking. "Please talk to me. I need to talk to you. Our baby needs you. Please don't do this to us. Don't do this to our son."

For the first time since the delivery, tears came streaming down from Elaine's eyes. "We don't have a son," she shouted. Martin was taken aback by the abrasiveness of her voice. Up until that day, Elaine had always been even tempered, but not anymore. She was dead serious, that much Martin could tell.

Martin stayed with Elaine all that day and the next. He had left the room only once. Elaine could not accept the fact that her son had been born with Down Syndrome.

Martin had delivered several Down Syndrome babies during his years in practice, and was well aware of the many emotions that followed - trauma, grief, denial, depression and, more often than anything else, guilt. Elaine easily fit into all of these categories.

Elaine's decision had been made long before Martin had a chance to talk with her. She just wouldn't listen to reason. She had decided not to acknowledge her son's birth at all. For all those concerned, her son had died.

There was no reasoning with her. Chromosomes were the cause of their son's abnormality, but Elaine would not hear of it. She was to blame. As far as Elaine was concerned, the subject was closed and would never be open for discussion.

But for Martin, this was only the beginning. He had a son and if it took forever, he would die trying to make Elaine understand that Stevie was their son and their responsibility. He could only pretend so long, especially when reality hit him like a bolt of lightning.

Two days later, Martin stood in the corridor of the maternity floor. He was holding Stevie in his arms, watching and hurting inside as the woman he called Sophie reached for his son and welcomed him to her life with a sweet kiss and a tender hug.

"Sophie," Martin said as his words swelled together, "Would it be alright with you if I came to visit Stevie every day?"

Sophie replied with a warm smile. "Dr. Lewis, Stevie is your son. You can visit him as much as you want. Twice a day if you need to. You're his father and you don't have to ask more than once. My home is open to you."

Martin and the woman exchanged a heartfelt smile. Martin leaned down toward his son and whispered, "Whatever happens in your life, I will always love you."

Martin had no idea that Elaine had been watching from outside her hospital room. She didn't expect him to understand why she had chosen to do this. She realized that Martin couldn't understand what he did not know. But still she held her past and private thoughts to herself.

Before she walked back into her room, she quietly mumbled to herself, "Stevie, I'm sorry."

In her dreams that night, she tossed back and forth. Her breathing began to get heavier. First she was hot, then cold. Tossing and turning, her teeth chattered. It was time.

The cemetery. The rain. Showering rain falling from the sky. Elaine laid herself on top of the grave. She was crying out to Stevie, "I don't want you to be dead. I'm sorry. Mommy's sorry. I love you…"

Maggie and Martin were still in the kitchen, just about ready to clean up, when a loud scream was heard throughout the house. It was Elaine. Another nightmare.

Martin ran up the stairs and into their bedroom. Elaine was sitting up, holding the covers to her chest. She was wet from perspiration. Her skin was flushed and her heart was racing. It was nothing unusual, but difficult to get used to.

Martin took Elaine in his arms. "Same dream?" he asked with deep concern.

Elaine was shaking. "Yes, the same."

Martin soothed her back with his fingertips. "If you told me about your dreams, maybe I could help."

"You can't," she shouted. "No one can."

"Elaine, please give me a try. I want to help you, really I do."

"I'm afraid no one can."

Chapter 4

In the morning, Elaine dressed quickly. That one last look in the mirror revealed glassy eyes caused by yet another unsettling night. As she opened her bag, she reached inside for her makeup case. This was a red lipstick day. It seemed to add hours of missed sleep to a somewhat colorless face. But she actually looked as wretched as she felt.

In the car, Elaine impatiently tapped the steering wheel to a nervous rhythm. Driving to Michigan Avenue from Glencoe wasn't easy, especially because the roads were once again going through massive repair, a staple of life in Chicago.

Elaine quickly pushed her way through the revolving door as if she had been in the medical building before. Taking long, deep breaths got her to the eighth floor. A new doctor always made her nervous. New questions, same answers. It was no wonder Elaine was panicked by the time she opened the door of the doctor's suite.

Seated behind the partition was an unfamiliar face dressed in a white uniform. "Can I help you?" she called out to Elaine.

"I'm Elaine Lewis, here to see Dr. Mitchell."

The woman behind the desk didn't smile, which made Elaine that much more uncomfortable. Elaine stood by the door, waiting for instructions. She was now at the crucial point. She wasn't sure if she should stay or go, but decided to stay.

It was beginning. Elaine's face paled as she looked into the partitioned window. Another unfriendly face walked right over to the window. Without looking at her, the woman said in a fast, rather matter-of-fact way, "Why don't you fill out the information form? Anything you don't know how to answer, don't. Wrong information is worse than none at all."

The nurse then disappeared and again Elaine was left with only the cheerless receptionist. There were other patients seated on the couch, but they weren't even looking Elaine's way. They didn't pay the slightest bit of attention to her. That was good. Elaine disliked small talk.

Elaine held the clipboard in her lap, filling out several questions, but certainly not all of them. The wait seemed like an eternity. Several times she looked at the door, but each time she started to get up, she sat back down. She had no choice, so she stayed.

Finally, another nurse came around the doorway. She not only had a kind voice, but she seemed to remember how to smile. "Mrs. Lewis, the doctor is ready for you now," she said, as she opened the reception area door for Elaine.

Elaine took a deep breath and straightened out her black, knit suit. It was the suit she always wore when she needed luck, and this day certainly applied.

She walked down the hallway, following the nurse. There were quite a few examining rooms, each filled except for the very last room. That was Elaine's room. It was equipped with the usual — magazines, a scale, a sink with a counter and, of course, the examining table with stirrups. There was also a small desk and a chair, which didn't look comfortable at all.

As Elaine looked around the room, she noticed several diplomas on the wall. But she already knew about that. Flowers, or maybe even several potted plants, would have worked better.

The nurse walked in and bent down beneath the examining table. She pulled out a clean, blue sheet, unfolding it as she handed it to Elaine. "Please don't start getting undressed until after you speak with the doctor. There are some magazines for you to read on the desk if you like."

In a while, an attractive, poised woman walked into the examining room. She held out her hand. "Hello Elaine, I'm Valerie Mitchell. Sorry to keep you waiting, but it's quite a busy day."

Elaine shook the doctor's hand but didn't speak. Dr. Mitchell sat down on the stool beside Elaine and took out her pen. "This won't take too long, but as I looked over your general information, I noticed several blank spaces."

Elaine sat back against her chair, listening as the doctor spoke. "Any relation to Martin Lewis?" Dr. Mitchell asked.

"Yes, he's my husband."

"We've worked together several times. Please give him my best."

"Dr. Mitchell," Elaine asked. "If it's all the same to you, could we keep this visit just between us? I haven't told Martin I was coming."

"If that's the way you want it, that's the way it will be. But as long as we have decided upon keeping this visit - and I presume any other visit - between us, I wonder if you would mind answering a few questions before the exam. It would be helpful."

Dr. Mitchell looked down at the clipboard, reviewing what Elaine had already scribbled in.

"Elaine, are you in reasonably good heath?"

"Yes, I am. Well, at least I think I am. I have been a little tired lately and maybe a bit more depressed than usual, but all in all I guess I'm not too bad."

Dr. Mitchell put down her pen, sensing quite a bit of apprehension. She stood up and grasped Elaine's hand. "Try to relax. Whatever is going on here, I will help you. It's going to be alright. You don't have to be afraid here. I have always observed my patients' rights, and I can assure you it won't be any different with you."

The doctor wrote down everything Elaine said on her clipboard. "One last question. Do you have any children?"

Elaine didn't answer, so Valerie asked her one more time. "Do you have any children?"

Again Elaine didn't respond, but this time Valerie tried to be a bit more persuasive. "This is really important. I understand you want your privacy, but I really do need to know. Was it a miscarriage?"

Suddenly, Elaine's voice turned cold and sharp. "It should have been. I'd rather not talk about it," she pleaded.

"Okay, that's enough for now. After your examination, we'll talk again."

During the examination, Valerie tried to keep the conversation going with small talk. But she stopped when she realized she was the only one talking.

When the exam was finished, Elaine sat up. Her face was pale and her heart pounded in frequent beats. She had several questions, but didn't ask them.

Valerie Mitchell walked toward the door and turned back to Elaine. "When you finish getting dressed, please come into my office. I think we should talk."

Elaine dressed in slow motion. She was in no rush.

Several minutes later, Elaine joined Dr. Mitchell in her office, which was large enough but not very attractive. No pictures, only framed degrees.

However, there was a certain softness in the doctor's voice that made her very likable.

As Valerie spoke, she watched Elaine's reaction, hoping she would somehow get to understand her new patient.

"Elaine, I don't know you well enough yet to know if the news I have for you is good or bad. I'm pretty sure you're pregnant, but I can't be certain without running a test on you. Before you leave, I'll need a urine specimen."

"Schedule an abortion," Elaine said without hesitation.

Dr. Mitchell was startled by Elaine's outburst. "Why don't we wait until we get the test results? You might feel better once you've discussed this with Martin."

"There's nothing to discuss. My decision won't change."

"Elaine, I've been practicing for many years now," Valerie explained. "Sometimes it takes time to get used to the idea of becoming a parent. Once you make the decision to actually go ahead with the pregnancy and learn about your baby, it can really be a great experience."

"I have no desire to be a parent, at least not anymore. When I was a teenager, I used to dream about holding and comforting my baby. Girl or boy, it didn't matter. I used to wonder what kind of mother I would be and if I really could love and receive love as a parent."

"It can still happen for you," Valerie added with enthusiasm.

Then the tears came. Dr. Mitchell just watched as Elaine fell apart. Valerie began to regret carrying the conversation that far, but she couldn't have known.

"Okay, Dr. Mitchell, I'll tell you why I can't and won't have a baby. I'm not exactly mother material. When the going gets tough, I bail out. I think you should know I had a son. He was going to be the best thing that ever happened to me. It was finally going to be my turn to give love. But everything went wrong.

"Six years ago, my baby, the baby that was supposed to be so special, wasn't special at all. In fact, he was born with Down Syndrome. I gave him to a woman I had never met. I hurt Martin, and for that I pay the price every single damn day of my life. I created a mess and walked away. Now Doctor, you have lots of different patients in your practice. What kind of a person does that make me?"

Elaine didn't wait for an answer. She stood up, ready to leave. "Tell me what I owe so I can be on my way. Give or take a day or so, and you won't remember me at all."

Valerie reached for Elaine's hand and sat her back down on the couch. "Listen to me for a minute before you walk out of my office and never come back. I will not pass judgment on you or, for that matter, anyone else."

Elaine began to calm down.

"You may not even be pregnant, but if you are, we can talk about all these decisions later. Let's take one day at a time. What do you say? Give me a chance to be your doctor. Whatever we say here is held in the strictest confidence. Please believe me. I want to help you. Don't be afraid of me."

Elaine sniffled her last tear. "Okay, I'll try."

Valerie seemed pleased, and continued. "Times have changed. Genetic counseling can help you get through your pregnancy. Give yourself a chance. Things do change."

"Maybe things do, but I can't."

***

Again Elaine had been late for dinner. She had phoned Martin right after her doctor's appointment, reassuring that dinner at Angelo's would be fine. What she didn't say was she planned to go to the racetrack that afternoon.

The reservation called for seven. It was eight when she arrived. Martin had already eaten his soup and salad when he noticed Elaine dashing toward the table. He was certain she had changed her mind about joining him, so he had already ordered.

Elaine kissed his cheek. "Hi, how are you?" she said, almost out of breath. She talked very fast, which indicated she was ready to tell a lie. "I'm so sorry. I was shopping and I lost my wallet. Just as I was about to retrieve my car from the valet, I realized I didn't have my wallet. As you can imagine, I was beside myself. I had to go back to the last dressing room I had been in. When I finally did come across my wallet in my coat pocket, you can imagine what a relief it was. So here I am."

Martin smiled. "Yes, I know you," he said, realizing this whole thing was rigged up by Elaine on behalf of her consistent tardiness. He knew she was lying but he didn't know why. Confronting her wouldn't help, so he didn't.

After dinner, Elaine excused herself and went to the ladies' room. She quickly tore up all the losing tickets from the track and threw them in the garbage. Then, for a second, she glanced at a note she had received from that same good-looking guy who owned the art gallery. The one she had said she didn't remember, but did. Elaine read on.

Dear Elaine:

It would really be fun to have dinner together, but if dinner isn't possible, that's okay. We can have lunch. If lunch isn't possible, we can meet for breakfast and if that's not okay, we can meet for coffee. If we can't have breakfast, lunch, dinner, or even a cup of coffee, at least please say hello to me when we see each other at the track. Or if you don't want to say hello, at least nod. At least I'll know you've noticed me.

Your whatever,
Josh

Elaine smiled. There was something about this man she liked.

***

In the morning, Elaine sat alone in the kitchen, waiting for the phone to ring. She was expecting Valerie Mitchell's call, giving her the test results. But they were merely a formality. She was certain of two things. She was definitely pregnant, and she wanted an abortion.

First she counted the tiles on the floor, then she looked up at the ceiling and counted the cracks. Then she poured herself another cup of coffee while she waited.

Finally the phone rang. Elaine picked it up after the first ring. "Hello," she said, sounding rather impatient.

"Elaine, is that you?" Dr. Mitchell asked.

"Yes, it's me. Well, am I …"

"How do you feel today?" Valerie asked with concern.

"That depends on what you say. Am I or am I not?"

"Yes, you are," Valerie explained.

There was an immediate, silent pause.

"Elaine, are you still there?" Valerie asked with concern.

Elaine remained seated, nervously tapping her foot to the floor. She wasn't shocked. However, hearing the words and knowing they were true made it all harder to accept. "Schedule the abortion. Please schedule it for me," Elaine said, trying not to sound as desperate as she felt.

"Have you mentioned anything to Martin?" was Valerie's next concern.

"No way. I just can't. I know what he'll say and I also know what he'll ask of me."

"Would that be so bad?" Valerie asked.

"You're damn right it would. I don't want a baby, not now or later."

"I will schedule the abortion for next week if you will allow me one indulgence. Please think this over. I know you're afraid, and I really do understand, but please just take a couple of days to think about it."

"If I do as you ask, will you do the abortion?"

"Yes I will," Valerie reluctantly agreed.

Relieved by Valerie's agreement, Elaine took a deep breath before ending their conversation. "Thank you for your help."

"I may not have to abort your pregnancy at all," Valerie clarified her decision.

With certainty, Elaine added, "Don't expect miracles."

"Miracles do happen," Valerie concluded with a lighthearted tone.

"Not to me they don't," Elaine finished with her usual approach. She hung up the phone and headed upstairs.

She was going out for the day to a place where nothing really mattered. Elaine dressed quickly. Black sweater, pants and shoes. Her clothes reflected her mood.

That day Elaine drove faster than usual, and almost passed the entrance to Arlington Racetrack. She attributed her nervousness to her phone conversation with Valerie Mitchell.

All the way there, Elaine had promised herself not to think about anything at all. She had hoped for a clear mind, which meant nothing short of angels with wings.

The parking attendant immediately approached Elaine as he opened her car door. Not knowing his name, she acknowledged him with a slight nod and a couple of bucks.

In the clubhouse, her table was ready. Her usual waiter had just placed a pitcher of lemon water down at her table. When she was seated, he poured her a glass of ice water and left.

Her mind, never clearer, anticipated a much better day than she had planned. Elaine could feel her heart beating slower and in a matter of minutes, she entered a much different world than the one she resided in. She wasn't Elaine Lewis or Dr. Martin Lewis's wife - she was just a woman betting on some horses. A woman who was excited by the races and indulged herself in heavy betting.

During the sixth race, Elaine could feel someone staring right through her. It was Josh Derman. She pretended not to notice him, but he knew she had.

Josh motioned for his waiter. When he spoke, he pointed directly to Elaine. "Please send that lovely lady this note," Josh said as he placed a white envelope on the waiter's tray.

As Elaine read the note, she couldn't help but smile.

To Elaine:

Well, what is it going to be? Breakfast, lunch, dinner or coffee? If you think I'll go away, you're wrong. I'm quite persistent. Or haven't you noticed?

Josh

Elaine reread the note. When Josh saw her smile, he assumed he might be able to get an answer in person. He walked over to Elaine's table, but before he could get a word out, Elaine spoke. "Please sit down. Is there something wrong? I have felt your eyes on me from the start."

Even though Josh would have enjoyed sitting right next to Elaine, he sat directly across from her. He smiled. "Okay, which one is it? Breakfast, lunch, dinner or coffee?"

"None of the above."

"Okay, then how about a cappuccino?"

"You are really a very funny guy," Elaine said as a certain sense of comfort came over her.

"I'd rather be known as handsome."

"You're that too." Elaine couldn't hide the blush that came across her face.

"Your innocence is refreshing," Josh added.

"I never really thought of myself as innocent," she said.

Josh grinned. "To me you are."

The ice had been broken. For the first time in a very long time, Elaine felt somewhat relaxed. She even laughed, which she rarely did.

Time passed quickly. The last race had just ended and the clubhouse was emptying out. Josh reached for Elaine's hand, certain she would push him away. The mere fact that she didn't gave him license to be just a bit more aggressive.

***

Martin would be late for dinner. However, Elaine wouldn't notice, because she would also be late.

As Martin approached Stevie's home, several thoughts mulled around in his mind, none of them original. Different day, same thoughts.

Heading the list was taking Stevie home for a visit. The next was telling his mother she had a grandchild. Finally, far more important than anything else, was hoping that Elaine would or could hug Stevie. Once she did that, the rest would be history. Down Syndrome was just words. Stevie was as perfect as any parent could hope for.

Sophie answered the door with her usual smile. "Doctor, you're early. Come in. Stevie will be right down."

"Is it okay?"

"Of course it is. Can I get you anything? Coffee, a cold drink, some of those chocolate-chip cookies you love?"

"No thanks. I'll save my calories for our trip to the Ice Cream Palace."

Sophie grinned. "Stevie has been talking about that place all day. He loves it there."

Martin laughed. "Me too."

"Like father like son," Sophie added as she walked toward the stairs and called out, "Stevie , your daddy's here."

There he was, thumping down the stairs, hurrying right into Martin's arms. "Daddy, Daddy! Ice cream, ice cream…"

Martin's face always lit up when he saw his son. "You bet, ice cream it is."

Martin gave Stevie one last hug before they went on their way. That was Martin's favorite part of their visits, the hugs and love they shared. Even if it was for only a couple hours a day, he and Stevie were stacking up memories never to be taken away.

The one thing Martin missed the most was tucking Stevie into bed at night and kissing his forehead, telling him everything would be alright. Kids need that. That's what Martin had done every day of Becky's life. God he missed her and Iris. He tried to let go of his memories of Becky and Iris, but after losing a wonderful daughter and loving wife at the same time, the memories were all he had.

Martin was just about to open the door when he turned back to Sophie and asked, "Can I bring you and the other children some ice cream?"

"That would be great. The other children would like that. Some of them don't get any visitors. Stevie is quite a lucky boy."

"Sophie, my dear, I think you've got that wrong. It's me that's lucky."

***

Dinner went well. Josh did the talking and Elaine did the listening. Surprisingly enough, on their way out of the restaurant, Elaine reached for Josh's hand. She held on tightly.

Elaine closed her eyes for a quick second, wondering if the queasiness she was feeling was because of the baby she was carrying or her immediate fear of the man who stood next to her. She was caught off guard as to why she felt instantaneous attachment to a man she barely knew.

As Elaine squeezed tighter, Josh couldn't help but say, "You don't have to hold on so tight. I'm not going anywhere, at least not without you."

"But I am," Elaine said as she started to let go of Josh's hand and walk alone.

"Why are you going? I assumed you were having as good a time as I was."

"That's not it at all. I haven't laughed like that in years. In fact, I really can't remember the last time I laughed."

"Then why can't you stay? Did I say something to offend you?"

"Josh, it's nothing like that. Nothing at all like that. I have a husband to go home to. In fact, I really do have quite a good man. I shouldn't have accepted your invitation to dinner."

"Then why did you?"

Elaine decided not to answer the question. She didn't know the answer, at least not just yet. She needed some time to get her thoughts together. Another man would only complicate matters.

Josh hailed a taxi. He held the door open for Elaine, ready to follow her in. Before Josh entered, Elaine stopped him. "I think we had better say goodbye now."

"Is this goodbye for the evening or forever?" Josh asked with an uncertain tone.

Elaine tried to be as honest as possible. "I really don't know. I wish I did."

Josh nodded in agreement. "Okay, if that's what you want. I don't want to upset you. You decide."

Elaine's eyes filled with tears. She softly whispered, "Thank you for a wonderful evening. You made me forget it all."

Josh seemed puzzled by her words. "Is that good or bad?" he questioned.

"That's very good. Yes, very good," Elaine answered honestly.

Josh leaned down and kissed her with all the sweetness any woman would remember.

***

It was nine in the morning. Martin sat on their bed, watching Elaine sleep. He smiled as he couldn't help but notice her peacefulness. Martin bent over and kissed her forehead not planning to wake her. But he did.

"I'm sorry," Martin explained. "You were sleeping so soundly, I didn't have the heart to wake you. Sleep is what you need."

Elaine peaked over to the nightstand and looked at the clock. "It's nine thirty. Why are you still here?"

"Late day today," Martin answered quickly.

Elaine was amazed. "What kind of late day? You never have late days."

Martin answered with a smile on his face. "Anniversary kind of late days. Did you think I would forget?"

"No, you never have, and I know you probably never will." But she had.

Martin walked over to Elaine and gave her a kiss. Her response wasn't exactly idyllic, but after her evening with Josh, she held back more than usual.

Martin didn't seem to notice her listlessness and if he had, he probably wouldn't have said anything. He had learned to accept Elaine's peculiar mood swings as the norm.

"Remember, dinner at the club tonight. Oh, before I forget, there's a little something under your pillow from me," Martin said on his way out.

As soon as Martin closed the door, Elaine reached under her pillow. She pulled out the black, velvet box that Martin had placed there for her. There was a small card attached to the box. Elaine read the note, "To our love."

For several minutes, Elaine sat there staring at the velvet box, trying to erase the previous night's dinner with Josh — the conversation, the laughter, all of it.

When she finally did open the box and took out the spectacular diamond-and-ruby bracelet Martin had given her, she was so ashamed.

Tears of confusion fell as Elaine held the bracelet tightly to her chest, repeating, "Martin, I'm so sorry. Really I am. I do love you."

***

Maggie had fixed breakfast for Elaine, but as usual, she didn't touch a thing except the black coffee. Elaine's appetite had never been generous.

Elaine took her coffee cup, walking onto the patio and into the garden. Maggie stood at the sliding glass door watching Elaine, wondering if she could ever take the place of Iris. Strange how one man could love two women so completely opposite.

Maggie was just about to start her housework when the doorbell rang. There stood Sally Braverman, as beautiful as the youthful model she had once been — skin as white as snow, eyes as blue as the sky and a smile that rarely quit.

Maggie invited her in. "Have a seat. I've just finished making those blueberry muffins you love."

Sally sat down at the kitchen table, happily eating what was definitely one terrific muffin. "If that boss of yours ever gets sick of you, or vice a versa, call me. I'll triple your salary," Sally joked.

"Sounds inviting, but I think I'm here for the entire run," Maggie said as she poured Sally a cup of coffee. "I've been with the good doctor far too long to ever think of leaving. This is home to me."

"Well, I tried. So where's that friend of mine?" Sally asked. "We have a day of beauty scheduled. I hope she hasn't forgotten."

"I think she might have," Maggie confided. "She's in the garden."

Sally seemed surprised. "The garden? Tell me she's planting seeds and I'll really be astounded."

"No, just walking around. Ms. Braverman, can I ask you something?"

"Of course, Maggie. What is it?"

"Have you noticed Elaine to be a little out of sorts lately?"

"I certainly have. That's why I planned this day of beauty. Especially because of tonight's surprise anniversary party. I'll tell you, Martin is one hell of a guy. Elaine's one lucky woman."

"You bet she is," Maggie acknowledged.

"Well, maybe after tonight she'll pep up. Every woman needs a little love and attention. But then again, if every woman had a husband like Martin Lewis, there wouldn't be divorces."

The patio door opened. Elaine seemed a bit dumbfounded seeing Sally sitting at the table.

Sally smiled. "Well, I guessed right. You forgot."

"Forgot what?" Elaine asked.

"Our day of beauty. Michigan Avenue calls."

Elaine looked at her friend. "I can understand me having a day of beauty. I look like a mess. But you, there's not a hair out of place. You're Chanel all the way — purse, shoes, jewelry, hat. You look perfect."

"No one ever looks too good. There's always room for improvement."

"Not for you there isn't," Elaine added. "You look terrific, but then again, you always do."

Sally stood up and gave Elaine a hug. "That's what I love about you. You actually think I'm better than I am. Flattery will get you everywhere, except out of today's day of beauty. Now be a good girl and get dressed. You know me, I'm a stubborn redhead who won't take no for an answer. In the meantime, I'll have another muffin while I'm waiting. What's another couple of hundred calories?"

"Calories?" Maggie joked. "There aren't any calories in these muffins and if you believe that, we can all retire on the money we'll make promoting these heavenly muffins."

Maggie and Sally seemed amused, but Elaine wasn't.

By two in the afternoon, Elaine and Sally had been wrapped and unwrapped in big, plush, terrycloth towels. Their faces were oiled, creamed and covered with thick mud packs. Their eyebrows were tweezed, shaped and conditioned.

Sally reveled. "What a pity this day has to end. I feel terrific. This is even better than chocolate cake. Well, almost."

During their last steaming, Sally crossed over the line. "Okay, now that you're feeling better, I have to ask you something. But if you don't want to answer, don't."

"Okay, go ahead. I'm listening."

"I guess I might as well get straight to the point," Sally admitted.

"This sounds serious."

"It is," Sally said, just a trifle apprehensive. "It's about Josh Derman."

"Josh Derman? What about him?"

"I think you've answered my question."

"Sal, what on earth are you talking about?"

"So you do know him?"

"Of course I do. You introduced me to him at his gallery. Remember?"

"I don't mean that. You know what I mean," Sally initiated.

Elaine seemed angered. "No, maybe you'd better tell me."

"Are you seeing him?"

"I had dinner together with him, but I am not seeing him the way you mean."

"Why dinner?" Sally questioned.

"Because he asked me to."

"And that's all?" Sally assured herself.

"Yes, that's all. Why the third degree?"

"I know it sounds like that, but really it isn't. I'm concerned. You happen to have one of the best guys around. So why Josh Derman?"

"There really isn't anything between me and Josh. You don't have to worry. And I do know Martin is a good man. Josh and I had a harmless dinner, nothing more."

"According to you it was harmless, but let me tell you, and I speak from experience. Josh Derman has been in one too many beds, including mine. He's quite a charmer, and that's all I'll say for now. Please be careful."

From the look on Elaine's face, Sally knew she had shocked her friend.

"Sal, don't worry. I'm fine. Really I am."

"But I'm still going to be worried. You are the last person in the world I ever thought I would be having this conversation with. As I sit here next to you, I think of you and Martin as a couple, a happy couple. What could have happened to change all that? Why another man?"

Suddenly there was a long, despondent pause. Elaine regretted not being able to confess to Sally about how Josh had made her laugh. For the first time in a long time, she'd had a peaceful night's rest. She didn't attribute it to Josh, but it was odd.

Their conversation was interrupted when the masseuse entered and stood boldly in front of them. She was a large-framed woman with a thick waist and legs that thumped as she walked.

"Ladies," she said with a drill sergeant's voice, "Didn't we say no talking? If you don't relax those tired muscles, those nasty little wrinkles will be with you forever. So what do you say we keep very, very still and, before you know it, this will all be over. Then you can talk. Got it?"

Both women nodded. Elaine was quite happy their conversation had been interrupted. She didn't want to confess her decision to see Josh again. Her heart had spoken.

Chapter 5

After beauty came reality. Elaine came home to an empty house. Maggie had asked for the evening off and Martin was finishing up his office hours.

Once again, Elaine was alone. She hated silence, since she always felt it caused loneliness. So with only herself to please, she turned on some symphony music. Loudly, of course. There was no other way — powerful music was comfortable for her.

Elaine glanced at her dressing table and noticed a small, white envelope with her name on it. She quickly read on.

Dear Elaine,

Don't forget our dinner date. The club at eight. Happy Anniversary.

Love,
Martin

Elaine started to get dressed. She glanced at herself in the mirror, then stood sideways, touching her flat stomach. Without thinking, she grabbed a pillow from her bed and stuffed it into her robe. Now she looked pregnant.

She closed her eyes and lifted her head back, almost trancelike. She looked into the mirror again, but this time she saw herself years before. She was just about ready to deliver. She reminded herself how fast those nine months really went by.

Elaine quickly pulled the pillow out from under her robe, wondering what the hell had gotten into her. Her decision to have the abortion would not be changed by her questionable feelings. Once again, she had proven to herself that making a decision and showing proper judgment were impossibilities. She often said one thing and did another.

She opened Martin's dresser and yanked out the bottom drawer. She threw everything on the floor and pulled out several pictures of Martin and Stevie.

She held the pictures close to her heart with remarkable attachment. With smooth movements, Elaine's fingers touched Stevie's face. As she closed her eyes, she imagined herself holding her son. Only God and her knew how deeply she cared.

Regardless of the years that passed, Elaine unwillingly had vivid memories of the night before Stevie would be leaving her. Rarely a day passed when she hadn't wished she could turn back the clock.

It was after ten. Stevie would be leaving the hospital in the morning. Not with his parents, but with a stranger Martin called Sophie.

Everyone on the maternity floor had gone to sleep, all except Elaine. She buzzed for the nurse.

When the night nurse entered the room, she turned on the nightlight over Elaine's bed. "What can I do for you, Mrs. Lewis? I'll be leaving soon and you need all the rest you can get. New mothers always need more sleep than they get."

In embarrassment, the nurse stopped herself from continuing the conversation. She had forgotten Elaine would not be taking her baby home.

There was a brief pause before Elaine asked, "Do you think it would be possible if I could see my baby?"

At first the nurse didn't respond. She had been confused by the question.

Elaine repeated herself. "Do you think I could see my baby?"

Finally, the nurse responded. "Are you sure about this?"

"Very sure. I just want to say goodbye."

It hadn't been more than five minutes when the nurse returned, holding the baby to her chest. She handed the baby over to Elaine, watching her reaction very closely.

At first, Elaine didn't look at her son. She just held him toward her breast in a nurturing way, gently rocking him as he began to cry.

Elaine looked up at the nurse. "Do you think I could have a few minutes alone with my son?" she asked.

The nurse hesitated, but then she agreed. "I'll be right outside if you need me. I'm not very sure this is such a good idea."

As soon as the nurse left, Elaine opened the blanket and, for the very first time, she looked at her son. She leaned over and kissed his forehead. "You smell so sweet," she said as she kissed his tiny hand.

Elaine held Stevie for quite some time before she spoke again. "I'm so very sorry for what I've done to you. This is all my fault. I love you and don't ever let anyone tell you I didn't. Have a good life, my baby. I love you."

Tears fell from Elaine's eyes as she handed Stevie to the nurse. "Could you please keep this visit between us?" she asked, confident that she would.

"If you wish." The nurse didn't look back as she left Elaine's room. It was not her place to judge or discuss Elaine's decision.

Elaine sat in the same chair until morning. When it was time for Stevie to leave, she watched from a distance, but she was there for the final goodbye.

***

When the phone rang, all thoughts of Stevie were erased. She answered with an awkward voice, "Hello?"

"Elaine, it's me, Sally. Are you okay?"

"Fine. I'm fine. Why are you calling? We barely just left each other."

"I know," Sally confessed. "But I felt horrible about carrying on about Josh the way I did. Can you forgive me?"

"Sure. Don't worry about it," Elaine said, imitating a nonchalant attitude.

Sally's voice indicated relief. "Okay, hon. I'm glad. Love ya."

Elaine hung up the phone and finished getting dressed. However, she had decided to make a stop before meeting Martin.

***

It was seven and Martin was counting the minutes until Elaine walked into the Lakeshore Club. He hoped he had made the right decision. Planning a surprise anniversary party was fun but a dangerous choice, knowing Elaine may or may not be happy about the celebration.

Coincidentally, just as the guests were starting to arrive was when Martin's stomach started fluttering. He paced back and forth, deliberating how this evening would really conclude. Realizing it was risky made it all the more ghastly.

When the maitre d' spotted Martin, he hurried over to him, talking while he walked. "Doctor Lewis, your wife just called."

At once, Martin stopped pacing. "My wife, why? Is something wrong?"

"No, not at all. She said she was fine. She especially wanted me to tell you not to worry, that she will be here but she will probably be late."

"Are you sure she didn't want to talk to me?"

"Doctor, remember, this is supposed to be a surprise and you weren't supposed to be here yet."

"Oh, right. Are you sure she's alright?"

"She said she was fine. Don't worry," the maitre d' added, trying to comfort him.

Martin's face turned pale. "Don't worry," he repeated. "I have no choice but to worry. Two hundred guests will soon be arriving. Are you sure she said she's going to be here?"

"Why don't you have a drink and try to relax? Everything's going to be fine," the maitre d' suggested.

"I wish I could believe that, but I have this sinking feeling in the pit of my stomach that tells me it won't."

Martin joined some of the guests, trying to make himself believe everything would be fine, but he knew he would never be able to convince himself. There was one certainty he could count on — tonight wouldn't be the night he had planned.

***

By the time Elaine had reached Josh's apartment, she had been in the midst of changing her mind. She got as far as the elevator and then, instead of pressing the button to go up, she walked straight out the door and head-on into Josh.

"Well, this is a surprise," Josh said as he gave Elaine a hug.

"A good one or a bad one?" she asked.

Josh smiled. "A very good one. But where are you going? The elevator is the other way."

"Well, actually I was just leaving."

Josh took hold of Elaine's hand and together they walked back toward the elevator. "I don't think so," he said. "No, I don't think so at all."

The moment the elevator door closed, Josh pulled Elaine close to him. "Why are you trembling?" he asked as he gently but passionately kissed her cheek, working his way downward.

Elaine responded with tears. "I don't really know. I don't even know why I came here in the first place. My husband is expecting me and I'm here with you. This entire picture is all wrong."

When they got inside Josh's apartment, Elaine sat down on one of the chairs next to the balcony. She looked outside at the beautiful view of the city and wondered just exactly what she had wanted or expected from Josh.

"Would you like a drink?" Josh asked as he poured a mineral water for himself.

"Do you have vodka?" Elaine asked.

"Certainly, what kind of a bar doesn't have vodka? But as I understood, you don't drink."

"Tonight I do," she added as she swallowed the vodka in one gulp, coughing afterward.

***

It was almost eight. The maitre d' walked over to Martin and whispered in his ear. "Are you okay?"

Martin whispered back, "No, I'm not, but I'm trying my damnedest to cope."

"I'm certain your wife will be here soon."

Martin faintly smiled at the maitre d'. "I really do hope so."

Martin stepped back inside the ballroom, which had been lavishly decorated in Elaine's favorite color, light blue.

The twenty-piece orchestra had started to play while the guests began to dance. The bar had been opened and the guests stared to mingle around the lavish appetizer table, which included the finest of cheeses, pates and fresh shrimp. Price had been no object when it came to pleasing Elaine.

Martin stood at the doorway, greeting his guests while at the same time looking down at his watch. His wish had been falling short of his plan, as did almost everything he had tried to do for

Elaine. All he wanted was one simple thing, Elaine's happiness. A sheer impossibility, he thought.

***

Esther Lewis had been looking for her son. When she spotted him looking out the window at the golf course, she came up to him from behind. "A limo. You never said anything about a limo picking me up."

Martin smiled and turned around. "Well, did you like it?"

"Like it? It was great. Like I was a movie star or something like that. There was a television and a bar. I even had a cup of fresh-brewed tea."

"I'm glad you liked it," Martin admitted.

Esther laughed. "Wait until I tell the girls at bingo. They'll probably think I'm lying, but oh well. What the hell, it still was pretty darn terrific."

Martin looked at his mother. "You look great tonight."

Esther pushed down on her dress, smoothing it out. "You think so?"

"You bet I do."

Again Martin glanced at his watch. It was past eight. He was getting nervous but afraid to show it. Conversing with his mother seemed like an adequate way to pass time. "So, how do you feel?" he asked.

"Good," she answered.

"Did you say good?"

Surprising herself, Esther answered, "Yes, as a matter of fact I do. Tonight I feel good, but tomorrow I might just be fair."

Martin kissed his mother's cheek. "That's the mother I've grown to love," he said.

By nine, Martin had begun to assume that something awful had happened. He phoned his home, but Elaine was not there.

He called his service, wondering if there had been a message for him, but there had been none.

He knew his ability to control his thoughts was shaky, and he was also aware that his imagination had a tendency to go wild. He had no choice but to make one last call before he panicked. He dialed the hospital emergency room. Too embarrassed to give his name, he gave an alias.

"Hello," he said. "This is Sam Lerner. I'm very concerned about my sister who did not arrive at my house on time. Could you please tell me if anybody named Elaine Lewis has been brought in?"

The rude young woman's voice on the other end said, "You'll have to wait until I find someone who can check it out. We're busy tonight, so if you'll hang on I'll try. But I can't promise you a thing, not tonight."

Martin's mind raced for the next few minutes when that same inattentive voice finally returned. "And you're waiting for?" she asked.

"Someone to check out the emergency room patients. I'm looking for Elaine Lewis."

"Oh, yes … I forgot. I'll be right back to you," she said in a hurried manner.

Finally, the woman returned to the phone. "There's no Elaine Lazar here."

Martin's voice grew angry. "Listen to me as I speak and please, if you will, write down exactly what I say. This is Dr. Martin Lewis and I'm concerned about my wife Elaine." Again he repeated, "Elaine Lewis is her name. I'm at the Lakeshore Club. If you have reason to call me here, please do it. Now have you got it all?"

"Yes, Dr. Lewis, I do. And I'm really sorry for keeping you waiting. I didn't know it was you," the now-apologetic voice on the other end explained.

"I'm sure you didn't," Martin added with a touch of sarcasm.

"Goodbye Dr. Lewis. I'll be in touch if something should come up."

Martin walked toward the reception room. He glanced at Sally, trying to get her attention. She hadn't noticed Martin until he came up behind her. He whispered, "When you have a chance, I need to talk to you."

Immediately, Sally backed away from a superficial conversation with yet another habitual, attractive man.

"Well that was fast," Martin said as he discreetly pulled Sally away from the guests.

"Believe me, I won't be missing a thing. When I get back, he'll continue right where we left off. We were right at the part where he tells me how his inattentive wife doesn't understand him."

All Sally had to do was take one good look at Martin and she knew something was wrong. "What's going on?"

"Are you aware of the time?" Martin asked.

Sally peeked over at Martin's watch. "Oh, my God, say no more. Elaine's late. I hadn't noticed."

"Sal, something's wrong, very wrong. She called the club earlier to say she would be late, but this is really late. The guests are getting anxious. I have close to two hundred hungry people waiting for dinner. I don't know what to do."

Sally recognized Martin's reaction. She had seen him like that only once before. The night of the accident. Iris and Becky were late for a dinner party and then the call came. They were in a car crash. Their bodies were beyond recognition. Right at that moment, looking into Martin's eyes, she saw the same fear.

Their conversation was interrupted by the maitre d'. "Telephone for you, Doctor," he said, pointing to his office. "You can take the call in there."

"Thanks," Martin said as he dashed to the phone.

"Martin it's me," Elaine said as she stood, nervously tapping her foot as she spoke. "I'm sorry about tonight. I know how much you love to celebrate our anniversary."

"You got that right. Where the hell are you? Are you alright?"

Elaine's voice lowered. "Well, I guess I'm fine."

"Then where are you? You're supposed to be here at the club."

"I know, but something came up."

"Such as?" Martin's voice demanded an answer.

"It doesn't really matter. Does it?"

"It sure does. I'm here waiting for you. Doesn't that mean anything to you?"

"Yes, Martin, it does matter. But we need to talk."

"Fine, we'll talk later, in private. Please. Tonight, just have a good time. Can't this wait?"

"No, it can't."

"Elaine, please don't do this tonight. Meet me here. I'll wait," Martin pleaded.

"No, Martin I can't. I'll see you at home."

Martin closed his eyes and meditated on his thoughts. He sat down as he waited for the click. Once again, Elaine had disappointed him. But why, he asked himself, did he keep trying?

After hearing the click, Martin stood up, trying to compose himself enough before telling his guests that the guest of honor was a no-show. He should have felt foolish, but instead he felt very happy. He had never questioned his love for Elaine, but sometimes love just didn't seem to be enough.

In a noble fashion, Martin walked to center stage and held the microphone tightly. "Well my friends, it seems as if the surprise is on me. I had planned this party for my wife without her knowledge and now, through no fault of hers, she is unable to attend."

The only sounds heard were the guests sighing in disappointment. They continued listening to what Martin had to say.

"But there is some good news," Martin added. "Everything has been paid for, so what can I say but enjoy? Dance till dawn if you want to and if there's anything you want, ask my friends at the Lakeshore. They'll accommodate you. I love all of you for being here and, once again, thank you."

Martin rushed out of the club, talking to nobody. Right at that moment, the only thing left for him to do was leave.

***

After her phone call to Martin, Elaine looked over at Josh and shook her head. "Sometimes, I really don't like myself at all."

"You might not, but I do. I really do," Josh said as he wrapped his arms around Elaine's waist, hugging her as he spoke. "I want to keep you here forever."

Elaine gradually pulled away. "I don't think so. It would only complicate matters. That's not why I'm here."

"Why are you here?" Josh asked as he sat down on the couch putting his head back.

"I'm not really sure. Tonight I came here because I feel comfortable with you."

"That's a start," Josh added.

"But I don't want another relationship that I can't handle. Don't you see? I can only bring you pain. That's all I'm good for."

"Did you ever stop to think we might be good for each other?" Josh added with credibility.

"No. Not really. I've never gotten that far."

"Well, maybe you should," Josh said as he stood up, inching his way toward her.

Again, Elaine stepped back. "Please don't confuse the issue. There's so much you don't know about me."

"As far as I'm concerned, there is no issue. Whenever a relationship begins, there's always a learning process that goes with it. What are you afraid of?"

Elaine's voice lowered, "Just about everything."

Josh took Elaine's hand and eased her beside him on the couch. "Let me tell you a little about me. Up until the day we met, I have always had a problem. For most men it really wouldn't be a problem, but for me it was. I had too many women. My friends used to joke around with me by saying if I didn't stop screwing every woman that came my way, my penis would fall off by the time I was fifty."

Elaine's eyes held confusion as she listened to what appeared to be Josh's confession.

"When I met you, something inside me changed. In fact, I think it was even before we were introduced. Something clicked into my distance mechanism. The one I always used to ward off any significant feelings. The one that kept me single and unable to fall in love."

"Why are you telling me all of this?" Elaine asked, not really certain she wanted to hear everything Josh had to say.

"Because I want you to understand you are not a one-night stand for me. I guess what I'm trying to tell you is I think I'm falling in love with you. Believe me, I'm plenty damned scared."

Elaine hesitated before speaking. "I really don't know quite what to say."

Josh moved closer to Elaine, desperately wanting to hold her after conceding feelings that did not come at all easily to him. "I really hope I'm not making you feel as uncomfortable as you look, but I just had to tell you how I feel."

The closer Josh inched in toward Elaine, the further back she moved. "Josh, please don't. Let me say what I have to."

Josh reluctantly did as she asked.

"You don't know a thing about me," Elaine said as she walked to the door. "I think it would be best if I left."

"Elaine, please don't go. I'm sorry if I made you this uncomfortable."

"I have to," she said. "This is all too familiar to me. A tense situation always causes me to run. It has become quite a habit these days."

With quite a sympathetic look on his face, Josh gently lifted Elaine into his arms and carried her to his bedroom. With the slowest and most tender of movements, their bodies melted into one. Elaine had decided to stay.

Chapter 6

It was after two when Elaine came home. Martin was sitting up in his favorite chair when Elaine stood before him in a somewhat apologetic way.

"What happened to you?" Martin asked. He was trying his damnedest not to lose his temper, but it became more difficult with every passing moment. "I have been pacing the floors for hours trying my very best to stay calm."

Elaine didn't know exactly where to begin. "I'm really very sorry, but tonight couldn't be helped. There are so many things going on in my mind that I don't even really know how to make you understand."

Martin couldn't help but put a stop to any more excuses. "Well, there's one thing I do understand. I planned a wonderful evening for you tonight and guess what? You didn't show."

"I'm sorry. Really I am."

Martin became angry. "Why don't you tell that to the two hundred guests who were waiting patiently for you to arrive. You were the guest of honor at our anniversary party. I even planned a ceremony for us to renew our vows. I thought if I could get you to feel comfortable with our life together, maybe you would tell me what the hell is going on here. Then, and only then, will our having been together really mean something."

Elaine's face turned a pale shade of white. "Oh my God. I had no idea."

"Exactly. That's the idea. It was supposed to be a surprise. It was quite a party. The band was terrific and the food was fabulous. The guests had a great time. What more could any host hope for, other than the guest of honor in attendance."

Elaine stood there for a long time without saying one word. She looked into Martin's eyes, which were filled with disappointment and hurt. Once again, she had hurt him. It was now one time too many. She had to do the right thing, which meant leaving him.

"Martin, as I stand here looking at you, I see a man with the highest of principles. I see a man with so much love to give. And then I take a good look at myself, and that's when I begin to wonder how does a woman like me get such a wonderful man?"

Martin listened as she spoke and then added, with a certain degree of certainty in his voice, "Don't immortalize me. I'm just like everyone else, or at least I want to be. I want what every man wants. I want a life I can count on. I want you to love me."

"Martin, I'm wrong for you. Can't you see that? I probably always was, but I guess I talked myself into believing everything would turn out the way it should be. But it hasn't. It never will. You know what I'm saying is true. Our marriage can't work."

Martin took several slow, deep breaths before asking the obvious. "Why can't it? We can get help. Together, apart, whatever you say. We'll do it together."

"I don't think so. You will be far better off without me. You can find another woman. A woman who can love you the way you should be loved. Every time we're out, especially at a hospital function, the single women, and sometimes even the married ones, give me that look."

Martin, astonished by Elaine's reasoning, asked, "What look are you talking about?"

"It's the look telling me not to turn my back, even for a minute. Believe me, once the knowledge is out about me leaving, you won't be alone for very long."

"I don't want someone else. Doesn't love count for anything?"

"Martin, take a good look at me, and I mean really look at me. If you don't know when to call it quits, maybe I damn well better."

Martin could see Elaine was under a great deal of emotional strain. At first he just watched as Elaine nervously walked upstairs. But when she slammed the bedroom door behind her and locked it, that was when he began to feel helpless and scared.

Martin stood outside of their bedroom, wanting to hold Elaine and tell her everything would be alright, but he didn't. Maybe it was his fault, he wondered, as he heard Elaine pulling out a suitcase from the closet.

She was going to leave him and now had to be the time to stop her. He knew once Elaine walked out that door, she might never return.

Martin banged on the door. "Please give me some time," he shouted. "Give me a chance to change your mind. Please Elaine. I don't want you to leave. At least open up the door. I need to see you. I can't lose you, not now."

Elaine answered back through the door, "You're not losing anything at all. I have nothing to offer you."

"Please open. I won't try to stop you, but let me see you," Martin begged once more.

Finally, Elaine gave in. She slowly opened the door and went to sit on their bed. Martin followed. He reached for her hands, which felt like ice. "Do you remember what I said to you right before we were married?"

Elaine shook her head, realizing she had remembered very little about that day.

"I told you that I had fallen in love with you for the good times, for all the bad times and for everything in between. This is in between."

"No, Martin, this isn't in between. This is all of it. This is life, that's all there is for me."

"I don't believe that at all," Martin said, trying to reassure her.

"Well, I do. Just let me go." Elaine stood up and continued to pack her suitcase.

Martin didn't say another word while she packed. But right before she was ready to walk away from their bedroom, Martin cried out to her. "I can't lose you. I know it's hard to love you, but I do."

Much to Martin's surprise, those were the words that stopped Elaine from leaving.

***

Once again, Elaine had decided to live a lie. Pretending she wasn't pregnant didn't change the fact that she was. She had talked to Dr. Mitchell several times since she had been to see her.

Each time, their conversation adjourned on the same note. Think about it. Which Elaine did, morning, noon and night. But still the same answer predominated. She would have the abortion.

For the next few days, Elaine tried to convince herself to have the baby. When the going got tough, she headed for the track.

She hadn't seen Josh at the track, which should have allowed her to concentrate. However, once she saw those horses start to run, her thoughts diffused. Actually, that wasn't all bad. Her mind had a chance to relax.

Josh called several times a day and a refusal accompanied each call. Maggie didn't confront Elaine about it, but long before

Josh came along, the two of them had reached an agreement. No questions asked. Elaine preferred it that way.

From out of the blue, Maggie had asked for the day off. Martin never vetoed anything Maggie asked for. So it wasn't uncommon for even a spur-of-the-moment decision to be made, as this one was. However, when Josh called, she wasn't there to buffer for Elaine, who had to answer.

"Hello," she said, alert to who was on the other end.

"Elaine, is that you?" the familiar voice asked.

"Yes, Josh, it's me."

"Thank goodness. I've thought of everything short of breaking down your door and kidnapping you just to hear your voice."

"I'm really sorry," Elaine said apologetically. "I didn't know what to say."

Josh responded in his usual, quick-witted style. "Hello would have been a good start."

For the first time in days, Elaine laughed. It felt good, she thought. Wondering why Martin had never made her laugh, or why she wouldn't acknowledge that he had.

"When can I see you?" Josh asked, imagining she would say no.

"How about tonight?"

At first, Josh wasn't sure he had heard right. "Is that a yes?"

"Isn't that what you were expecting?" Elaine asked, certain she had surprised him.

"No, but that's the answer I wanted."

Elaine had begun to feel a little guilty, but what harm could be done? Martin wouldn't be home anyway. "Where shall we meet?"

"How does my apartment sound? I would love to cook for you."

Elaine paused for a moment, realizing it did matter where. "No, I don't think that would be such a good idea," she said quickly. "Neutral territory would be better."

Josh answered quickly, to ensure Elaine would not change her mind. "This isn't exactly a peace conference, but okay. Neutral would be fine. How about Blueberries? We'll dance."

"Dance? I haven't been dancing in years," Elaine answered with a smile.

"Good, then it's time you had. Meet me there at eight. Goodbye," Josh said as he quickly hung up the phone, afraid Elaine would change her mind if he didn't.

Elaine entered Blueberries at nine. The main room was filled with smoke and loud conversations. For a moment Elaine had thought about leaving, but when she noticed Josh sitting patiently on a bar stool, she knew she was caught up in his world.

At a glance, Josh saw Elaine and hurriedly walked her way. "I wasn't sure you would come."

"Me either, that's why I'm late," was her excuse. She walked back to the bar with Josh.

Josh smiled as he spoke. "I really am very glad you decided to join me."

Elaine smiled rather than say what she had been thinking. Which was how attractive he looked and how when he spoke to her, his voice really did excite her.

She was attracted to him in every way. But at the same time, she was frightened. Frightened of how quickly she had fallen for a man she barely knew.

That might have accounted for her drinking that evening. After a few drinks, Elaine didn't think about why she was there, only for how long and where they would go later.

Without asking, Josh lured her to the dance floor. He took hold of her waist and pulled her as close to him as possible. It was as if they were making love right there in front of everyone.

Later, at Josh's apartment, Elaine had begun to cry. Josh picked up on her sadness and the fact she had a bit too much to drink. He immediately tried to help. "Why are you so hard on yourself?" he asked.

"Why would you think that?" Elaine questioned, shocked by his accuracy.

"Because I see the pain behind your smile."

"There's so much you don't know about me," Elaine said as she started to get up from the couch, but tripped.

Josh took hold of her hand, not letting go. "Yes, that is true, but I want to know everything about you. What kind of child you were. Your parents, your friends, whatever. I want to know you."

"I don't think you would really want to know me. There's quite a bit of my life that I wouldn't discuss with you or anyone else. So you see, knowing me wouldn't really be very good for you. I'm not a very good person. I've made a lot of mistakes, some I would change and some I wouldn't."

Josh eased in, realizing he had hit a sore spot. "Me too. My life hasn't really been a bed of roses either. But whose has?"

Suddenly, without notice, Josh started to undress her. He slowly unbuttoned her shirt and slid his hands across her belly. She tensed up, wondering if he knew he was touching her baby.

Elaine didn't try to stop him, so he made love to her without ever knowing she was pregnant.

Elaine wasn't sure exactly how she had gotten there, but she awoke in Josh's bedroom. Josh was still sleeping. So as not to wake him, she slowly got out of the bed, tiptoeing into the bathroom to shower.

When Josh awoke, Elaine was seated on the window ledge, looking outside as far down below as she could see. She was covered with a large, terry towel.

"Isn't it a great view?" Josh asked as he reached to his nightstand for a cigarette.

Elaine didn't answer. Instead, she asked Josh with tremendous sincerity, "Have you ever wished you had never been born?"

Josh, puzzled by her question, responded, "No, never. Have you?"

"Yes, every single day," she candidly responded.

***

It was five in the morning when Elaine came home. Martin was sitting on the hallway stairs, waiting for her. "Where the hell have you been?" Martin asked as he watched Elaine kick off her shoes.

He startled her. "Oh, Martin, it's you. I didn't expect to see you until tomorrow."

"I guess not. I decided to drive in tonight instead of staying in Wisconsin."

"Martin, I'm sorry, really I am."

"Well, are you going to tell me where you were?"

For several lengthy moments, Elaine sat staring at Martin in a very non-committal way.

By the time she decided to answer Martin, he was halfway up the stairs. He had convinced himself that Elaine was not about to explain her whereabouts. He did, however, smell a trace of hard liquor on her breath. But he didn't mention it.

"Martin," Elaine called to him. "I love you, really I do."

Martin didn't respond. Instead, he just kept right on walking up the stairs, recognizing a couple of hours' sleep would be better than none.

Elaine knew he wouldn't return when she heard their bedroom door close. That night was the first time Martin had ever let things ride. Usually a discussion would follow, in which Elaine would fabricate a story of where she had been and why. But not that night.

***

Later that day, Elaine called Valerie Mitchell's office. When she answered, Elaine quickly blurted out, "Dr. Mitchell, this is Elaine Lewis and I have made my decision."

"And that is what?" Dr. Mitchell asked, already knowing the answer.

"I'm going to have the abortion. Please schedule it as soon as possible. I will call you later. Please don't wait thinking I'll change my mind. The decision has been made by me and me alone. I have not told Martin about the baby, and I'm not going to."

***

In the afternoon, Elaine went to the racetrack. Arlington was very busy that day, so Elaine sat in the grandstand. She didn't want to bump into anyone she knew, and it would be highly unlikely that her immediate group of friends would be seated there.

During the third race, Elaine placed the largest bet she had ever made. "Guess you feel lucky today," a voice from behind whispered.

Elaine turned to the voice. "Hello, Josh."

"Surprised?" he asked as he took hold of her arm, walking her back to the grandstand.

"A little," she replied. "I assumed you were the clubhouse type."

Josh smiled. "Actually, I'm not. In fact, I enjoy being closer to the horses. I was raised on a farm. I know I don't look the part, but if I have my choice, just give me some open space, clean air and a pair of riding boots. That's my heaven."

"Not exactly the metropolitan lifestyle you lead," Elaine said as she sat down on a bench. "You do run with a rather fast crowd."

Josh smiled. "You're right, I do, but it's that fast crowd that helps me pay my family's bills."

"A family?" Elaine asked, again surprised by his unpredictability.

"Oh yes. I have a mother, father and two brothers, one of whom is severely handicapped. The bills are outrageous, but Mom refused to place my brother Scott in a home. She has devoted her entire life to him and, if I might add, she did quite a remarkable job with him."

Josh noticed as Elaine's face grew pallid. "Are you alright?" he asked as he grasped her hand.

"I'm fine. It's just a little warm and I haven't had a thing to eat all day."

Josh stood up. "I can fix that."

It was a strain, but Elaine smiled and said, "That would really be nice."

While Josh was gone, the third race began. Her horse lost and so did she, five thousand dollars. Almost in a daydream, Elaine stood up. Without batting an eyelash, she placed the losing tickets on her seat and left.

When Josh returned with a sandwich and a cup of coffee for her, he found the losing tickets torn up in pieces on the seat. Much to his dismay, Elaine had vanished.

Chapter 7

It was late afternoon when Martin arrived at Sophie's. Stevie was out in the yard with the other children when Sophie called out to him. "Stevie, your daddy's here."

In a split second, Stevie raced inside, still out of breath from volleyball. "Daddy, Daddy! Hello, Daddy, hello!"

Martin opened his arms and in flew Stevie. That's the way it was every time Stevie and Martin were together. They shared a special love.

Sophie marveled at the response Stevie gave his father. Watching the two of them was such a pleasure. Especially the way Stevie looked at his dad. It was beautiful. Their premium relationship was not to be matched with any other child-parent relationship Sophie had ever seen.

When Stevie's excitement eased up he asked, "Ice cream, Daddy? Ice cream?"

Martin looked at Sophie. "I have an idea."

"Okay, Dr. Lewis, I'm listening," Sophie replied with curiosity.

"What about getting the other children ready and we'll all go out for dinner?"

"Are you sure about this, Doctor?"

"Absolutely. I'd love it," Martin assured her.

While Sophie got the other children ready, Martin and Stevie went for a walk. As they walked, Martin couldn't help but hope Elaine would someday change her mind and the three of them could be a family. Unlikely as it seemed, Martin could still dream.

Dinner went well. Noisy, but well. It wasn't about what the children ate or even if they liked the pizza. It was that they had a chance to mainstream with others. That's what made their outing so important.

It was after nine when Martin and Sophie finished bringing in all the children and got them ready for bed. Martin was the only parent who assisted her in any manner what so ever. Nothing was ever too difficult for him.

Some of the other children had never felt the tenderness and warmth of an adult other than Sophie. Most of the other children had visitors only on birthdays and holidays, if at all. But when Martin was there, he made them all feel special.

He would say to hell with the parents who dropped their children off with Sophie, expecting no responsibility. He knew what a sin that was. But maybe, just maybe, somewhere along the line some of the parents would come to understand that their children needed to be treated just like any other child. If only they would try. That included Elaine.

Once in a while, Martin insisted Sophie take a few hours for herself. On those days, he and his nursing staff would pinch hit for her. The time away made her job less difficult.

That night as Martin was leaving, Sophie handed him a package. "Now Doctor," she said, "I know how you hate thank yous, but cookies, that's different."

Martin smiled as he opened the package and looked inside. "You've found me out." Even before he was out the door, he reached inside the cookie tin and took one out, happily biting into it.

By the time Martin reached home, he was getting tired. The kitchen light was on, so he entered his house through the garage.

He wasn't expecting Maggie to be home, but he was glad she was. "I thought you would be gone at least another day," Martin said as he sat beside Maggie, who had also been nibbling on a cookie.

They both sat at the kitchen table, nibbling and conversing for what seemed like a very long time. Martin yawned a few times, but he wasn't ready to go upstairs.

"Why didn't you stay?" Martin asked with great concern. "Did something happen?"

"No, nothing unusual. My sister and I can't be under the same roof for very long. Strange things happen to us. We revert back to our childish behavior and all hell breaks loose. It's just not worth it."

Without asking, Maggie reached for another glass and poured Martin a glass of milk. It was habitual for Maggie to care for him.

"Thanks, Mag. What would I do without you?"

"Starve? Yes, you probably would."

Martin laughed at the truth.

"Is everything okay?" Maggie asked, conscious of the fact Martin slightly sugarcoated the truth.

"Oh fine. Everything's fine. And you? How did it go with your aunt?" Martin asked.

"Pretty good, but I wanted to get back here as soon as possible. You know how families can be. Once I'm there, I'm ready to get back here. Sometimes it's quite funny to watch two old women fighting about the same things they fought about when they were children."

"They say people never really change, they just get older," Martin added.

Maggie looked at him in her straightforward, no-nonsense way. "Are you sure everything is alright?"

"Really, I'm fine."

Maggie acknowledged her disbelief. "Oh sure, I can see that. I bet you haven't slept in days."

"I can't fool you. Can I?"

"Nope, you can't and you never will."

"Mag, is Elaine home yet?"

"Yes, she's been home for quite a while."

"Good. If you'll excuse me, I think I'll go upstairs and check on her."

Martin stood at the foot of their bed with a desperate desire to make love to Elaine. She was so beautiful when she rested.

He quickly removed his shoes and socks. Then he sat on their bed for several minutes, afraid Elaine wouldn't respond to his desperation. A quick and disturbing thought occurred to him. What if she pushed him away? Could he understand her dismissal once again? He couldn't bear the thought of rejection, at least not tonight.

Martin was just about to get in bed when Elaine opened her eyes and said, "I was waiting for you but I fell asleep."

"Me? You were waiting for me?" Martin questioned.

"Yes," she whispered. "I was waiting for you."

Martin eased his body down next to Elaine's. His hands trembled with desire, afraid of the closeness that might only last for moments. Sometimes, he was afraid to get close to her, knowing that when morning came, she might be gone.

After several minutes of kissing, Elaine moaned in sheer excitement, which she had never done before. Martin's desire grew stronger and, for the first time in a very long time, Elaine was a part of him.

Elaine kissed Martin with an urgency that had never been present before. Old memories were gone from their minds. There were no pressures or unpleasant thoughts lying beside them. Tonight it was only Elaine and Martin in their bed. They were finally free, if only for a few unplanned moments.

In the morning, Elaine was no longer a part of Martin. Once again, she felt alone.

Chapter 8

It was late afternoon when Elaine left a message for Dr. Mitchell. "This is Elaine Lewis with an important message for the doctor. Could you please tell her to hold up on the abortion plans? I need some more time."

As the hours passed, Elaine's confusion continued. She couldn't make any decision. In fact, she couldn't even think. She was quite upset. Having nowhere to go, she drove to Arlington Racetrack.

She took the elevator up to the clubhouse, but when she entered the dining room, she immediately turned around and left.

Before leaving, Elaine sat on a bench near the entrance. She closed her eyes and tried to think of something pleasant — anything at all — but she couldn't.

"I didn't think you were coming today," Josh said as he sat down beside her.

"Please Josh, I really need to be alone today."

"That is precisely why I won't let you," Josh said with authority. "You need a friend."

"No, Josh, that isn't what I need."

"Then what is it you do need?"

"That I don't know," Elaine said as she stood up to leave.

Josh grabbed her hand. "Please let me help you."

As the minutes passed, Elaine was getting more upset. "What are you doing here anyway? Why are you always here?"

"And why are you always here?" was Josh's sharp response.

Elaine shouted, "I don't know."

Josh took hold of her hands. "I'm here because you're here. You remember our chance meeting? Well, it wasn't a chance meeting at all. From the very moment I laid eyes on you at the gallery showing, I wanted to find out as much about you as I could. I had never even been to the racetrack before meeting you. All I wanted was to be a part of your life."

Elaine was astounded by his honesty. "I had no idea this was going to be so serious for you," she said with sincerity.

"Isn't it for you?" Josh asked, hoping for the right answer.

"Yes, it's serious, but I have a husband I love. But then there's you. I hate myself for having the feelings I have for you. I keep hoping my feelings for you will disappear. It's the wrong time for us."

Elaine left the racetrack alone while Josh stood there watching her leave, unable to stop her.

***

Elaine drove around the city for hours before she decided to call Martin. She stopped at a service station with an adjoining diner. Reaching into her bag, she pulled out some change, which fell to the ground.

Her hands were trembling and thoughts were passing in and out of her head faster than she could retain any memory of them. She was scared, but determined not to become hysterical.

Martin answered on the first ring. "Hello," he said in a panicked voice.

"Martin, it's me."

"Where are you?" he asked with tremendous urgency.

"I'm not exactly sure."

"Elaine, please come home."

"I can't, at least not right now. I'm having trouble getting my thoughts together."

"Let me help you," Martin pleaded.

"I wish you could, but it just isn't possible."

"Let me try. I'm your husband for God's sakes. Just tell me where you are and I'll come get you. No questions asked, I promise."

Elaine paused for a moment to think. "No, I think I need to be alone. Please just give me some time."

Martin hesitated for a moment before insisting. "Elaine, tell me where you are and I'll be there. You've got to come home."

"I don't think I want to. Not now."

Hours had passed since Elaine had called. If only she would walk through that door, Martin promised himself he wouldn't ask any questions. He would be so dammed glad to see Elaine that nothing else would matter.

He hoped he would remember that thought, but somehow he knew he wouldn't. His anxiety would overpower any previous promises. That was the usual scenario.

At four in the morning, Elaine checked into a motel somewhere off the highway. Her decision to stop driving became obvious when her eyes began to close as she approached a tollgate.

She should have called Martin, but she didn't. Instead she went out to the car, opened her trunk and pulled out two bottles of Absolut vodka. She closed the door to her motel room and began to drink.

Elaine slept for several hours before she began to dream. When her dreams turned into horrifying nightmares, she awoke. It was time to call Martin.

She was still slightly hung over when Martin answered. "Hello, Elaine is that you?" he asked in a distraught, overtired voice.

"Yes it is."

"What is going on? You're drinking, aren't you? You're self-destructing. Let me help you. I want to bring you home."

"That won't be possible. I really don't know where I am."

Once their conversation ended, Martin tried to reflect on how this could be happening. Every reason led him to another theory.

He took his time as he walked into the kitchen. He was hoping the pains he now felt in his chest would go away. Reaching into his pocket, Martin took out a small vial and opened it up. He slid his medication under his tongue, certain he was alone.

But he was wrong. Maggie stood watching, waiting for an opportune time to question him. When she recognized the relief on Martin's face, she asked with concern, "I think it's time to tell me what's going on here. And don't sugarcoat it like you always do."

"It's just a little heart problem. No big deal. With medication I'll be fine."

"Are you sure you're telling me the truth?" Maggie asked, prepared to be supportive.

"Yes, that's all this is about," Martin reassured her. "It's just a minor problem. Angina, everyone has it."

Maggie gave him a look. "Everyone doesn't have it. We need to talk, so cut the crap."

***

Elaine entered the diner surprised to see a full house, mostly men. She hadn't put on a drop of make-up — she hadn't even glanced at a mirror. She could only hope she didn't look as bad as she felt.

Sitting next to her was a rugged but well-groomed man, probably about forty. Most men seemed ageless to her. "Morning," he said in a friendly manner.

At first Elaine looked the other way. He then repeated his greeting in the same, friendly way.

This time Elaine responded. "Morning."

For several long, silent moments, neither spoke. Elaine, who had never been much for small talk, strongly wanted this stranger to talk to her.

Unexpectedly, the silence was broken by Elaine. "Are the eggs good?" Elaine asked, not giving a damn either way.

"They're pretty good, but the pancakes are better," he said as he pointed to the man seated next to her. "See, that guy eats pancakes every day, damnedest thing. I've been coming here for over a decade, and Gerald over there has never had anything different. A little boring, don't you think?" he added with a chuckle.

When it was obvious that Elaine wasn't going to laugh, the man responded. "Sorry about that. Yes, you'll like the eggs," he said, answering her original question.

Elaine nodded as she motioned to the waitress, indicating she was ready to order. The conversation with the man beside her had ended by her choice.

After four cups of coffee and horrible eggs, Elaine paid her check and left. She had no idea the man sitting next to her at the counter had followed her back to the motel.

The key had already been in the door when the man called out, "Wait, miss, you forgot your handbag." She looked down at her hand. He was right.

"Thank you very much," Elaine said as the man handed over her bag.

"Do you play poker?" he asked.

"Sometimes," was her answer.

"Good, we need an extra," he said as he held out his hand, prepared for a handshake. "Mac Porter here, and you are…"

"Elaine Lewis," she said with just a tinge of reluctance. Talking to strangers was contrary to her beliefs.

Then she reminded herself of Josh. He was also a stranger. She was concerned by her morality or lack of it, and of how drastically she had changed.

Instead of saying goodbye and going inside, Elaine followed Mac back to the diner and down a full flight of stairs.

Her eyes immediately focused directly on the poker table in the middle of the room. There were decks of cards and stacks of chips in the center of the table.

Her excitement intensified as she eagerly awaited her chance to play the game. She was ready even after promising herself it would never happen again. This was just another example of a promise she couldn't keep.

Seated around the table were five men ranging in age from late thirties to mid-forties. They weren't particularly good-looking, except for Mac. He had a powerful build with deep, brown eyes and an easy smile. Somewhere between his calming voice and his friendly handshake, she felt comfortable with him.

One of the men, the balding one with the hoarse voice, called out, "We're ready whenever you are."

Realizing his buddy may have offended Elaine, Mac whispered to her, "Don't pay any attention to him, he hates women." Mac laughed. "I'm just kidding, he has a wife and six daughters, but what he doesn't have is patience."

Before being seated, she looked around the room, not finding what she was looking for. She turned to Mac and asked, "Is there a ladies' room, restroom, bathroom - whatever you call it here?"

"It's upstairs. Go ahead, they won't start without you."

"They?" Elaine asked. "Aren't you playing?"

"No, I hate cards. That's why we're always looking for another hand."

"Oh," Elaine said. "I guess I shouldn't be flattered. It's almost like you picked my name from a hat. I suppose anyone who checks in is fair game."

"No, only the ones who can afford to lose."

Elaine's eyes widened. "And just how in the hell do you know that?"

Mac thought for a moment before answering. "Promise you won't get mad?"

"No, I'm fine," Elaine said, as she stood tapping her foot on the floor.

"Your car. Anyone with a Jaguar these days has a few bucks. If you stay here, in this rather remote place, it's because you don't want to be found. Am I right?"

Elaine didn't answer. Instead she walked upstairs to the bathroom, thinking about what Mac had said. She had all the intensions of leaving, but she didn't.

While Elaine played cards and the hours passed, Martin sat by the phone, waiting for Elaine to call.

In the morning, Martin left at six. He had several patients to see that day and canceling office hours had never been his style.

Even after Iris and Becky's deaths, when his life was in agonizing limbo, he had patients to think of. He went to work each and every day, refusing to wear his sorrow on his sleeve. That's what made him the envy of most, his loyalty and the ability to care about others first.

***

Elaine had begun to feel sleepy. She looked across the table at men she didn't know or want to know, wondering why the hell she was sitting there. Three years had passed since the last episode of non-stop card playing.

That game lasted three days, but Martin had been out of the country. Then she only had Maggie to contend with. Elaine was certain Maggie never believed her story. That's when the wall between them began.

It was eight when Mac returned. Elaine had become so engrossed in the game that she hadn't noticed him leave.

"Coffee anyone?" he shouted as he came barreling down the stairs with a large thermos.

The card players, including Elaine, didn't respond. "Maybe you should call it quits," Mac whispered in her ear.

Elaine looked into Mac's eyes with a despondent and tiring stare. "I'm perfectly fine," she said with a grin.

Mac finally caught the attention of one of the guys and motioned with his head to end the game. The balding guy responded with a head shake, meaning no.

Mac sat on the couch by the wall, watching the game. He couldn't help but wonder why this game had lasted so long. This had never happened before.

Finally, the game ended. Elaine had lost ten thousand dollars.

Mac remained downstairs with Elaine as the others staggered upstairs for something to eat. They were all tired, but only Elaine seemed weakened. Maybe it was caution, or maybe it was guilt, but Mac stayed with Elaine until she decided to leave.

It was only a second or two before Elaine had the key in the door when she passed out. Mac carried her into her room and stayed with her for the entire day.

He had been a medic in Vietnam and had not held a woman in his arms since his last day of duty. That was when a woman he helped drag off a field died in his arms, just as he had pulled her to safety. Shortly after his discharge, Mac had a breakdown.

Elaine would be different, he thought as he watched her sleep. She was far too beautiful and soft, untouched by sorrow. He didn't know her pain and she would never know his.

When Elaine finally did wake up, Mac was there. Elaine nervously lifted the blanket she had been covered with up toward her chest. "What happened?" she asked.

"You passed out," Mac answered.

"During the game or after?" was Elaine's next question.

"After."

Elaine put her head back against the headboard, trying to remember some of the details. "I lost, didn't I?"

Mac lit a cigarette before answering. "Yes, you did. Quite a lot, I might add."

"How much?" Elaine asked, biting her lip as her memory started to return. Her eyes widened as she recalled the men at the table. "Never mind, I'm starting to remember."

Before Mac sat down at the edge of the bed, he motioned for Elaine's approval. "Is it okay?"

She nodded. "Did we, you know, sleep together?"

"No, we didn't."

Awkwardly, Elaine cleared her throat before speaking. "Oh..."

"Who's Stevie?" Mac asked.

Elaine took a long, silent, deep breath. "Why do you ask?"

"You called out his name several times."

Confused by her subconscious she answered, "Oh... he's just someone I know."

"Well, now that you're up, how about something to eat?"

Again Elaine sat in silence. Then without warning, she blurted out, "Why the hell do you do this to people?"

Mac hesitated for a moment. "I don't know. It seemed harmless, that is until now. I don't think I'll be doing this again. I really have no right to ask this, but can you forgive me?"

Elaine was surprised by his words. "I don't think it will matter either way. Tomorrow you'll probably forget that I even existed."

"I don't think so," Mac said, shocked by the discovery that he had meant what he said.

"Well I do," Elaine said in a confident manner

"You learn a lot about a person by watching them sleep," Mac added, certain he had.

Mac had become frightened by his thoughts. He felt an awakened response to feelings he thought he had lost. They were strangers, this couldn't happen. But it had and Mac didn't know exactly how to handle his emotions. It had been years since he had felt anything.

"I'll be right back. You need some nourishment," Mac said as he opened the door and headed back to the diner.

Elaine stared at the phone for a very long time before dialing. She was relieved when the answering machine picked up her call.

After listening to the message, she chose her words carefully. "Martin, I'm doing okay. Not great, but good enough. Remember when I told you I wasn't worth all the aggravation? I'm certain by now you would agree."

By the time Mac had returned with her breakfast, she had showered and put on lipstick. Mac placed a tray of food on the dresser.

"Voila," he said as he lifted the top of the tray. "Well, let's see what we have. Orange juice, oatmeal, toast, jelly and, oh yes, coffee."

Elaine walked over toward the tray and poured herself a cup of coffee. "Thanks."

Before biting into the toast, she looked down at the tray, noticing a second cup. At once, she started to pour Mac a cup. "Cream, sugar or both?" she asked.

"None for me, thanks. I guess they gave me an extra cup. I've already had my breakfast. As usual, I had breakfast at five thirty. That's my starting point."

"What about ending?" Elaine asked.

"My day doesn't really begin or end in any specific way. I wake up, do whatever and then I go to sleep, or at least I try to sleep. Actually, that kinda sums up my life."

Elaine didn't respond until she had finished her breakfast. She was hungrier than she ever remembered. Probably her nerves, she imagined.

"I appreciate your kindness, but isn't your wife wondering what happened to you?"

Mac hesitated for a moment. "There is no wife, no family, just me. No cat. No dog. No bird. Not even a goldfish. So you see, nobody will miss me. What about you?" Mac asked, anticipating there was no husband.

"No, just me," she answered, adding one more lie to her memoir.

For the next few minutes, neither of them spoke, each knowing what was about to happen.

Mac took one long, deep breath before he could even look Elaine's way. Slowly, he walked toward Elaine. They did not touch each other. Their eyes met. He hesitated for a moment.

Mac's heart was racing faster than he had ever remembered. He desperately wanted to touch Elaine. She sensed the anguish Mac was feeling. They understood each other's pain. Deliberately, she cradled her head into his trembling hands. They held onto each other for a very long time before their lips met.

A tear fell from Mac's eye. Elaine wiped it away with the softness of her skin as she tried to soothe away any sadness he was feeling.

Carefully, Mac lifted Elaine toward the bed. It only took a moment before they were surrounded by the warmth of each other's bodies.

Elaine gazed into Mac's sensitive eyes. She felt safe when she looked at him. It was as if nothing bad had ever happened to her. For a moment, she had forgotten everything that stood between her and happiness.

Mac felt the passion rise as he held onto Elaine, afraid to let go in fear she would disappear. He caressed her face, desiring her in every way. He thought she was just perfect.

Sweetly, they had shared the most obvious of pleasures. They had both reached out to each other and were met by tremendous intensity. It was so much more than just passion. It was a friendship like neither had nor would again. For a short time, they were released from their private hell.

Their last kiss would be one to remember.

***

Driving home, Elaine started to feel ashamed of her behavior. She had never been promiscuous as a teen or as a young adult. In fact, she was just the opposite. Martin was the first man she had ever been with. So why now, she asked herself. Good God, she thought, a pregnant woman carrying on like this was nothing at all.

Trying to focus on this baby she was carrying was impossible. She couldn't seem to think past the next five minutes.

As she drove up to the house where all this godforsaken turmoil started, she gunned the car and kept right on driving. She circled the same few blocks for at least an hour before she finally stopped the car.

Elaine took a look at herself in the mirror. Her eyes were at half mast. She opened them wide enough to get a better look at herself, and didn't like what she saw. With unconscionable disgust, she spit into the mirror.

Again she tried to focus her thoughts on her pregnancy, but she couldn't. She started the car and drove directly home.

She was prepared for another confrontation with Martin. But there wasn't one. He was home, but instead of initiating another argument, he said nothing at all. Neither did she. At some point, she would have no choice but to explain.

Chapter 9

Several days later, Martin took Stevie and a two of his friends out for hamburgers. This time Sophie stayed at home.

Just as Martin was about to pay the cashier and get the boys back home, he felt a tap on his shoulder.

Turning around, he smiled as Sally greeted him. "Why hello there, old friend. I haven't seen or heard from you since the party. What gives?"

At that same moment, Stevie stood beside Martin, tugging his jacket and pointing to the shelf below the cash register. "Daddy, gum. Daddy…"

Sally was speechless. Martin shrugged his shoulders, uncertain of what to say.

"Martin, what's going on here?" Sally asked with a strong sense of confusion.

Martin held on to Stevie's shoulders, pointing him in Sally's direction. "Stevie, meet Sally. Sally, meet my son Stevie and his friends, Sam and Billy."

Sally warmly smiled at the boys. "Hello Stevie, Billy and Sam." Then, with a long, inquisitive look, she focused her eyes on Martin. "Your son, oh my God, Martin."

Martin didn't know exactly how to begin. "Well, Sal, as long as you two have finally met, why don't you come with me while I drive the boys home. That is, if you're done eating and won't mind."

"I just came in to grab a quick cup of coffee but that can wait. Something tells me this is a lot more important than a cup of coffee."

"Good, I'm glad," Martin said. "I'll explain on the way back."

Much to Martin's surprise, once he had began the story, he didn't hold back. When he spoke, Sally listened, and she cried when he did.

"Sal," he said with a sigh of relief, "I should have told you sooner."

Sally's response was direct. "You sure the hell should have. Maybe I could have helped."

Martin nodded and said, with extreme sincerity, "You probably could have."

That night he made a decision. Something had to change. In fact, that was exactly what he said the moment he saw Elaine.

Elaine was sitting in his office. They said their hellos and nothing more. All that could be heard was the wall clock and its offbeat, rhythmic movements.

Martin walked over to the large picture window behind his desk. When he needed answers other than the obvious ones, he would look outside and answers came from out of nowhere.

At once he turned to Elaine, not sure if he should hug her or question her. It was time to stop hugging and get some answers.

"Elaine, I really think we have quite a bit to discuss. Don't you? I don't think either of us meant for this to happen. Something has got to change, right now, tonight."

That was the beginning of a long night.

Elaine didn't take her eyes off Martin the way she usually did. She faced him and spoke in a straightforward voice. "You're right, but I really don't know where to begin or if I can."

Without her consent, tears began to trickle from her eyes. It was time. Elaine's hands tightened as she placed them in her lap. This time, regardless of her apprehension, she was going to follow through. Maybe Martin could forgive what she couldn't forget.

Martin backed off. Fear was rapidly causing him a great deal of anguish. Was he pushing too hard? Should he stop Elaine before her strength became diminished by the truth? There were too many questions and too many reasons why he should stop her, but he didn't.

Instead he reassured her. "Don't worry, just tell me the way it is. I love you and whatever you tell me will not stop me from loving you."

Elaine paced back and forth for the longest time before beginning. "It's those damn dreams. I hate them. They won't leave me alone. Night after night I am reminded of my failures," she said.

Elaine began to shake as the unsettling images she had focused in her mind began to take over. Her voice was filled with sadness as she spoke. "You just don't understand how much I loved Megan. Nobody did."

Martin listened, bewildered by a name he had no knowledge of. He wanted to interrupt, but he didn't. He assured himself all the pieces would fit somewhere along the line.

Elaine continued. "I know I've never mentioned her before. I've wanted to, but couldn't." Then, with all the boldness that remained in her, she shouted, "Megan was my sister and I killed her." Elaine threw her hands over her face. "There, I've said it. I killed my sister. Yes, I was the one who did it."

Martin didn't know what to say. He wanted to comfort her, but suddenly his body froze. He didn't move, he just listened, wondering how it had been possible to delude her inadequate feelings for such a long time.

Elaine cried out bitterly as she proceeded. "It was August third. The hottest August third in Ohio since the records were being recorded. I had just turned seventeen that summer. Megan was twelve and a half.

"It was a day like any other. I was babysitting Megan as always. I loved her so, even with all her handicaps. Megan's limitations never stopped us from having a good time. We had each other and that had to be enough. We were sisters, but more than that, we were friends.

"Mom worked seven days a week while dad drank seven nights a week. Most of the time, dad never even came up for air, but we survived.

"We had been sitting on the porch for a very long time before Megan began to get hungry, thirsty and a little impatient. I didn't care. I was used to catering to all her needs."

Suddenly, Elaine stopped talking. She closed her eyes for a minute before continuing. She forced herself with determination to follow through.

Elaine's speech pattern began to accelerate as she proceeded. "She promised to stay on the porch... she promised." Elaine's eyes were filled with tears, deciding if she could go on. At that moment, her energies seemed wasted by her most horrible memories.

She sat down on the couch and crossed her legs, first to the right, then to the left. She was becoming overly anxious and very uncomfortable, desperately wanting to stop the charade. But she had come too far to step back to square one.

"She promised to stay on the porch with her dolly while I got her lemonade and cookies, her favorite foods. I kissed Megan's cheek and whispered, 'I'll be right back. Don't move.'

"Megan was capable of following directions as long as you gave them to her one at a time. So I waved goodbye and walked back toward the kitchen. It couldn't have been more than a minute or two when I heard brakes skid and then there it was, that horrible, screeching noise.

"After the screech came the silence. I ran out the door. The cookies and lemonade were airborne. I screamed 'Megan .... Megan ..... are you okay?' I knew she wasn't going to answer, but I called out to her anyway.

"By the time I reached the street, the truck driver who had hit Megan was beside her. I pushed him out of the way and I laid Megan's head on my lap. She was gone. There was nothing I could do.

"When I looked up, all the neighbors were standing on the street. Right before the ambulance came, I ran off."

Martin sat there, listening to every word Elaine said. He was overwhelmed. Pieces were beginning to fit and suddenly Elaine's behavior became obvious based on her trauma.

Elaine stood in front of Martin, her eyes enlarged as she spoke. "Don't you understand? A part of me died on that day. Megan and I weren't going to grow up together. It wasn't supposed to be that way. It was my fault. I never should have left her alone."

Martin motioned for Elaine to have a seat beside him. She couldn't, so she paced the floor as he spoke. "Didn't your parents reassure you? It wasn't your fault. It appears that you were quite a competent companion to your sister. She was very lucky to have you."

Elaine's voice raised an octave or two. "Lucky to have me? I don't think so. I killed her."

Martin thought the situation over again before asking, "Are you telling me that your parents said nothing to you? You were a young girl who did what you thought was best. What more could anyone ask for?"

Elaine caught her breath for a moment. "They never had the chance to tell me anything. That very evening, I ran off to Chicago."

"Why didn't you ever tell me about any of this before?" Martin asked with grave concern. "Things might have been different. I could have helped you through this."

Elaine answered with a strained voice, "Maybe so."

Realizing Elaine's exhaustion, Martin's anticipation of answers declined. He wasn't sure exactly how much Elaine could handle. She had appeared quite distraught and the last thing Martin wanted was to push her over the edge. There was always tomorrow.

That was when Elaine stopped holding back. It was shortly after dinner. Elaine sipped on her coffee as she tapped her fingers nervously on the dining-room table. Their conversation was very mundane — the weather, the news, whatever they did that morning - neither listening to what the other said.

Suddenly, Elaine stopped stirring. For a long, uncomfortable moment, Elaine watched Martin gazing her way in silence.

"Martin, I know all the harm I've caused you and all the changes in your life you've made for me. I really am so very sorry. I never meant to hurt you. Last night when I looked into you eyes, I could see all the damage I have done and how unkind I've been in my own selfish way."

Martin interrupted her. "Obviously, you have been sheltering me. But now, for the first time in a long time, I am beginning to understand why our life has been this way. All I ever really wanted was for us to know each other. If it meant sharing unpleasant memories, so be it. Life is what it is."

"I've tried to talk about it before, but I just couldn't," Elaine's voice grew louder. "I tried to make believe if I never said the words out loud, the pain would go away."

Without the slightest bit of justification, Martin walked over to Elaine, trying to embrace her. However, it was quite obvious to him that she was uncomfortable. He immediately backed off.

Elaine was beginning to lose control. She nervously paced back and forth. "Don't you get it? I'm a mess. I think it would be best if you wouldn't try to stop me from leaving."

"I don't want you to leave. Let me try and help you through all of this."

"Martin, I know you mean well, but you can't change what has happened in my life. I've tried to set the record straight, but even that didn't work."

"What did you do?" Martin asked with deep concern.

"I went back home. It occurred to me that whatever happened so many years ago might be looked at in a different way."

"So what happened?"

Elaine continued in a cold, matter-of-fact way. "I was too damn late. Mom had died shortly after I left, and my father suffered a severe stroke a month before I returned. Two days after I arrived, Dad died. Once again, I had left Ohio tied to my past."

Martin's voice held sympathy. "I'm really sorry," he said, coming to the revelation he really couldn't help her.

"It's not your fault. In fact, you did more for me than anyone else could have. When I met you, immediately my world became a much happier place. I should have known good things don't last, especially for me. Stevie was born and my world was once again topsy-turvy. I wanted a child so badly, nothing would have mattered. Well, that was what I thought. God wouldn't let this happen to me again, but he did."

Martin wanted to interrupt her, but he didn't. He was afraid Elaine would stop her confession. So he just listened.

"I couldn't take the chance of getting hurt again or hurting anyone," Elaine added with honesty. "I didn't want to be responsible for another tragedy. I was terrified I would kill my son the way I killed Megan. I couldn't let that happen. Death was all around me. I smelled it everywhere. I couldn't do that to my baby. He had to have a chance."

Elaine sat back down and stirred her coffee cup with strange but cautious moves, making certain she didn't tip over her cup with her trembling hands.

In a harsh tone, Elaine blurted out, "Well, now that you know everything about my life, does it change anything?"

Martin answered as honestly as he could. "No, I still love you. There isn't anything you've told me that makes me love you any less. I just feel closer to you."

Elaine lashed out. "Great. You feel better, I feel worse. So now what?"

Martin eased into his plan. "I think if you have some help, you might be able to work through all of this."

Elaine gazed at Martin in despair. She didn't speak, but just sat there as the wheels of her mind churned and reworked all her painful memories. She had begun to feel helpless and out of control.

She closed her eyes, desperately trying to find a core to focus on. Her mind began to spin and she was now unaware of which thought came first. They all seemed to be joined together by her confusion.

Suddenly she became dizzy and unaware of her surroundings. The room began to spin. Subconsciously, her thoughts filtered to Mac. Why Mac, she thought. He was only in her life for that one time. But would that be enough? He was different, special, and she loved him. Maybe she did. Her mind was so filled with chronic thoughts. Now what?

As plain as day, almost as if he were right beside her, Josh appeared. His image focused crystal clear. His gentle kisses and his powerful words were holding her together right at this crucial moment. She was losing her perspective and she knew it.

She opened her eyes and looked at Martin, who had been watching her. Certainly, he couldn't read her mind. If he had, it would have been horrible. She suddenly hated him. Then, if that wasn't bad enough, she actually gave into the idea of hating Stevie. She hated everything, but most of all, she hated herself.

Without warning, all hell broke loose. Elaine grabbed her half-full coffee cup and tossed it at the mirrored wall. She then randomly tossed several dishes, cups and silverware on the floor. "Damn everything. I hate everything and everyone!" Then she picked up the crystal saltshaker and threw it across the room and knocked over a lamp.

Just as Martin reached over to grasp onto Elaine's hands, trying to calm her, Maggie ran in.

"Oh my God," Maggie yelled as she started to clean up the mess. "What's happening here?"

Martin, quite shaky from the entire incident, tried his best to keep a level head. Tears fell from his eyes as he gathered Elaine in his arms. He began to realize there was so much more going on here than he imagined.

Without even a moment's hesitation, Martin looked at Maggie in desperation. "Please get me my bag."

By the time Maggie returned, Elaine had somewhat quieted down. Martin reached into his bag and took out a syringe. Still holding Elaine, he filled the syringe, tapping out the bubbles. Then, without hesitation, he injected her.

Several moments later, Elaine became relaxed and very sleepy. With Maggie's help, Martin slowly walked Elaine to the den and placed her on the couch. From the moment Elaine's head touched the cushion, she slept.

In the morning, Martin sat down beside Elaine. He brushed aside her hair as he whispered to her, "Please let me help you."

When Elaine finally awoke, she had no recollection of the night before. She tried to lift herself up from the couch but she felt achy and exhausted. "Why am I here?" she asked.

That was when Martin realized she had remembered nothing at all. "You were very tired. In fact, you nearly passed out, so in lieu of trying to get you upstairs, Maggie helped me bring you here."

"Thanks," Elaine said, taking that to be the truth. "I would like to go upstairs. Maybe I have the flu or something like that."

"Maybe," Martin said, finding it easier to agree.

"Will you help me up?" she asked.

"Sure, just hold on to my arm."

As they walked up the stairs, Martin couldn't help but feel concerned. It seemed unlikely that their life together would ever be in harmony. He was finally beginning to perceive that Elaine was under a great deal of emotional strain. So was he.

***

Later that day, Martin decided the time was right to speak to Elaine. Actually, he was aware that the subject matter he planned on discussing would never be something Elaine would readily accept.

Awkwardly, he cleared his throat. "Elaine, I have made an appointment for you with Jack Flemming. He's a good doctor and I think he can help you."

"I know I have several things to work out, but I can do it myself. Really I can. I don't need a psychiatrist. Just give me some time. I promise, I'll be better," Elaine said with extreme sincerity.

"Elaine, this is not a punishment. This is only to help you. Please do this for me."

Elaine's voice was forced. "Martin, please listen. I know what this is all about. It's about Stevie, isn't it?"

"Well, of course it has something to do with Stevie. Everything I do has something to do with Stevie. He's our son, and you're my wife. I love you both."

As the conversation continued, Elaine's uneasiness started to present itself. "Martin, maybe it's time for me to explain a couple of things to you," she said as she rubbed her hands up and down her legs, unable to unwind.

Noticing Elaine's uneasiness, Martin intercepted. "It's okay, it's not really necessary to explain your actions. Not to me. I'm not judging you now or for anything you've done in the past."

"I can't understand why not."

"It's simple. I have never sat in judgment concerning anyone else."

"And it's just that simple?" Elaine asked in disbelief.

"For me it is."

"Not for me," came Elaine's negative response. "You might not be perfect but you're a hell of a lot closer to heaven than I'll ever be."

Martin questioned Elaine's statement. "Now why on earth would you say something like that?"

"Because it's true. I know you have given Stevie plenty of love. I know about your daily visits, the ice cream, the pizza dinners, the zoo trips and everything else you and the children do."

"How would you know about this?" Martin asked with extreme curiosity.

"I've followed you many times," Elaine confessed. "I know about the pictures in your dresser. I know about all of it."

By the look on Martin's face, Elaine knew he had never suspected or had any knowledge of her following him.

"You were there? You've seen the pictures, all of them?" Martin asked with utmost interest and slight irritation.

Elaine responded with a nod. "Yes, several times."

"You saw Stevie?" Martin asked, completely astounded.

"Yes I did, and by the look in your eyes, I can tell for the very first time you do not approve of my actions. So maybe, just maybe, you are judging me and you have never realized it."

"I don't know what to say," Martin admitted.

"Neither do I," Elaine responded with concern.

Martin didn't say another word. Instead he handed Elaine a slip of paper.

She read it out loud. "Dr. Jack Flemming, tomorrow at two." She put the paper in her pocket and nodded in a positive way, with absolutely no intention of going.

Chapter 10

In the morning, Martin left for the hospital as usual. He was a bit apprehensive about Elaine insisting to see Jack Flemming alone but he agreed. After all, she wasn't being held captive. He believed her, which was his first mistake.

Elaine stood at her bedroom window, waiting and watching Martin as he pulled away. She felt a certain sense of dishonesty, but that didn't last any longer than it took to dial the phone. She had decided to call Mac.

After three rings, Elaine felt unsettled, so she quickly put the receiver down and went back into bed. She laid there for what felt like an eternity.

Closing her eyes, she saw the image of herself nine months pregnant. She could feel the pain and the shifting of her body as she dropped down to the floor. Something had gone wrong.

As she tried to get up, she could feel the pressure manifest itself. She silently screamed as she looked down on the floor to a pool of blood. There was not going to be a baby.

Elaine's imagination was quite vivid. After a while, she brought herself back to reality, and once again dialed the phone. This time it wasn't Mac who she dialed, but Valerie Mitchell. She let the phone ring until the doctor's service answered.

"Please tell Dr. Mitchell that Elaine Lewis will be in her office at six tonight." Not waiting for a response, she hung up.

She dressed quickly. With only a passing wave, Elaine said goodbye to Maggie. Elaine had gotten used to Maggie's watchful eyes. Her loyalty to Martin was incredible.

In a short while, Elaine grew tired of driving. She stopped for a quick cup of coffee and to use the phone. Once again, she dialed the number she had earlier reneged upon. Wondering what to say to Mac when he answered made her feel very uneasy and extremely unsure of herself.

Just when she was about to hang up the phone, someone answered but did not utter a sound. She could hear breathing and desperately tried to get the person's attention. "Mac, please, if that's you, answer me. It's Elaine. I want to talk to you. Please say something."

***

Elaine was right. It was Mac who had answered, but he didn't speak. He was afraid of what he might say if he responded.

Later, his mind wrestled with thoughts of her. Despite the promise they made to each other, he wanted to see her again.

Day after day, he constantly reminded himself of how, after returning from Vietnam, he had aided in his wife's departure. Nancy leaving him for his best friend was the frosting on the cake. No one ever prepared for that.

After that, he signed himself into the V.A. hospital. Three years later, his anger changed into understanding, but he still could not love or be loved. It was too late. Nancy had remarried. There could be no turning back.

Emotions and passion were only memories for Mac. His fear of closeness became a part of his life. He held any relationship he encountered at a distance. He revealed himself to no one.

It was understandable that the feeling he had been carrying with him since he met Elaine frightened him. Despite his fears, he decided to make the call.

Maggie answered the phone after two rings. "Hello," Mac's voice cracked. "Hello?"

"Hello," Maggie responded, not recognizing the voice. "Can I help you?"

"Elaine Lewis, please."

"Mrs. Lewis isn't home. Can I take a message?"

Mac's uneasiness caused him to panic. In one swift motion, Mac hung up the phone and ran out of the phone booth.

At that moment, he decided to never try that again.

Chapter 11

Driving was when Elaine did most of her thinking and the majority of her crying. There was something quite soothing about listening to symphony cassettes, but the beauty of the music made her sad.

Once the memories were brought out in the open, they remained with her for quite some time. Today was just like that. She couldn't seem to let go of any of her thoughts, even her more painful ones.

She had created quite a maze. She was immersed in a cocoon of anguish that she had brought on herself. She didn't know how to release her feelings and make a decision. Clearly she could not continue this way.

Everything was getting mixed up in her brain and confusion had become a way of life. There were Martin and Stevie to contend with, and all the mistakes she had made. Then there were Josh and Mac and the feelings she had for them. But the most painful and pressing was what to do about the baby she was carrying.

Things were so out of sequence there was no way she could put anything in its proper perspective. However, seeing a psychiatrist was out of the question.

Suddenly it dawned on her. She was wrong about herself. She could make a decision. She just did. The hell with Dr. Flemming and the hell with everyone. She turned the music up and headed for Arlington Racetrack.

***

At the track, Elaine sat at her table for several minutes before her usual waiter surfaced. As he stood by her table, he had already begun to write out her order.

"Same as usual, Mrs. Lewis, crab salad?" he asked.

"No, not today. I think I'd like to try something different." She stared at the menu, knowing she was not in the least bit hungry and had no intention of eating whatever she ordered. But once again, she made a decision.

"I'll have this," Elaine said as she pointed to the roast chicken.

Her waiter responded with his usual. "Very good decision."

"What would you say if it wasn't?" Elaine asked.

"Probably nothing."

The first race had not begun, so Elaine people watched in the clubhouse dining room. She especially couldn't seem to take her eyes off those who were laughing, wondering if she would ever be so mundane as to laugh like that.

***

Six o'clock came and went. Instead of being at Dr. Mitchell's office, Elaine was waiting outside Josh's art gallery.

Elaine reminded herself of her friend Sally's warning as she watched Josh, leaving the gallery with a tall, beautiful blonde whose arm was attached to his. They were certainly more than friends.

Not only was Elaine disappointed, but her uneasiness began to make her heart beat faster. That's when she pressed her foot down on the gas pedal and sped away. She didn't care if she made a scene or not. She had no intention of ever seeing Josh again.

Somehow she couldn't bear to see him with another woman. She thought that was quite strange, because she really didn't give a damn about him.

She talked to herself as she drove. "Damn it Elaine, you're so stupid." At the stoplight, she looked up at herself in the mirror and, with tremendous honesty, shouted, "G- d I wish I was dead. I wish I was dead…"

She patted her stomach for the umpteenth time, recognizing she was still pregnant. She was just as confused as ever.

At nine, she drove to Dr Mitchell's office. It was as she suspected. The lights were out and there was no one there. She questioned herself if that was really what she wanted.

At ten, she pulled into a gas station and bought herself a Pepsi. After that, she sat in her car for several minutes before walking over to a phone inside the station.

The attendant didn't even nod as she walked by. She reached inside her bag and took out her wallet for some change.

First she dialed Martin, but hung up. Then she dialed Sally, but the line was busy. Then Mac, Josh and Martin again. After that, she walked over to the candy machine outside. She bought a Snickers bar and some Raisinettes. She opened her bag and threw in the candy.

Several minutes later, she redialed Martin, Josh and Mac. After dialing each number, she hung up before the second ring.

Finally, after three Pepsis and six candy bars, the gas station attendant came over to her. "Miss, what seems to be the problem?" he asked.

"Problem? No problem, no problem at all. Really, sir, no problem," she said in a somewhat hysterical tone.

Suddenly she began to cry as she ran off into her car. She left with no idea of where to go. She just drove.

At midnight, she drove back to Josh's. She didn't call because she hadn't planned to go there. Some things just happened.

The doorman announced her not because she had asked him to, but because it was now an apartment rule. He refused to break it for her, even after she slipped him a twenty. He was as honest as Martin. Martin never broke rules, he just followed them.

"Why did you pull away like that?" Josh asked as he stood at the doorway, waiting for Elaine to get off the elevator.

Elaine thought before answering. "I don't know."

Josh grinned. "Maybe you were just a little bit jealous?"

"Jealous? No, I don't think that's what it was."

"Well, I'd like to think it was," Josh said as he motioned for Elaine to have a seat.

Elaine sat down and looked around the apartment. The last time she was there it was very dark and all she saw was the bedroom. But not tonight. She had not come there for that, though exactly why she was there was a mystery to her.

Josh closed the door and sat down next to her. "You're too much of a lady to ask me, so I'm going tell you. The blonde who I was with was one of my first girlfriends who, if I might add, is now my best friend's wife. They have three great kids and I am their legal guardian if something should ever happen. So, I'm innocent."

Elaine drew a silent breath, feeling relieved.

Josh moved closer and tightly held onto Elaine's trembling hands. "I think I'm falling in love with you."

Suddenly, Elaine felt she would scream if she didn't leave. It was getting hard for her to breathe. She stood up and, before Josh could say another word, she was gone.

***

It was after one when Elaine returned home. She had expected Martin to be waiting for her, but instead Maggie sat in the living room sipping a cup of tea.

There was no anger in Maggie's voice, just concern. "Are you okay?" she asked, taking another sip of tea.

"Yes, I'm fine. Where's Martin? What's happened?"

"There's nothing wrong," Maggie reassured her. "Martin had to pinch hit for one of the doctors. He had to give a speech."

"Where?" Elaine asked.

"In Wisconsin. He'll be home tomorrow."

Elaine nervously asked, "Does he know about tonight? Did he call?"

Maggie shook her head. "No, this is just between us."

"Thank you, Maggie. I know you must hate me. God knows I've certainly given you enough reasons to. In spite of all that, I still want to thank you for not telling Martin. You're very loyal to him."

Just as Maggie began to speak, Elaine stopped. Not wanting to be rude, she turned toward Maggie and, in a rather appeasing way, added, "It's okay. You don't have to say a thing."

"Goodnight Mrs. Lewis."

"Goodnight Maggie. Oh, and by the way, don't you think it's time you called me Elaine?"

Maggie nodded in good faith. "Goodnight Elaine."

For the first time since the awkwardness of their initial meeting, there seemed to be a slight bond occurring between the two of them.

Two messages were on Elaine's nightstand. She picked both of them up and read them. One was from Valerie Mitchell and the other was Mac. She returned only Mac's call, but there was no answer. At that time, the only thought going through her mind was that it was probably for the best.

*****

Elaine drifted to sleep. At exactly three in the morning, she awoke in a sweat. Her pillow was drenched from the horrors of her nightmares. It was happening again, but this time Martin wasn't there to give her comfort.

That's when she decided to call Josh. The phone rang many times before he answered. "Hello? Hello?" he said in a groggy, overtired voice.

"Josh it's me, Elaine. I have to talk to you. Can I come over?"

"Now? Are you sure? Do you know what time it is?"

"Please, I need to. Is it okay?"

"Of course it's okay, but I'll pick you up. This isn't a great time to be alone. Wait for me outside. I'll be down at the corner. I'll flash my headlights twice. This way your husband won't see me."

"That won't be necessary. Martin's out of town and I'm very capable of getting there myself. But you could do me a favor."

"Of course. What...?"

"Call down to your doorman and tell him to expect me."

"You got it."

Before leaving, Elaine placed a note for Martin on the foot of their bed.

***

Josh did as she asked. The doorman greeted Elaine as if he knew where she was going. She liked it that way. It made her less self-conscious.

Josh already had the coffee brewing when she arrived. "I thought we could both use this," he said as he poured them each a cup. "Somehow a good cup of java makes it all seem better."

"I don't think so, not this time," Elaine said in a very downcast voice. "Nothing can help me. I'm such a damned mess."

Josh took Elaine's hand and eased her over to the couch, trying to make her feel comfortable. He had sensed she was far too tense for any jokes.

Elaine sat motionless while Josh handed her a cup of coffee. "Drink this. You'll feel better."

Elaine quickly took a sip but then, with an abrupt movement, she put the cup down, stood up and began to pace back and forth. She did this for several minutes before she could say anything at all. Then it all came tumbling down.

"You know," she said, "I hate myself and I bet you have no idea of how that feels."

Josh interrupted. "Maybe not. But that doesn't mean that I won't be able to understand your pain. You know, all my life I've played around, never being there for anyone or, for that matter, never really needing anyone. But I want to be there for you."

Elaine laughed smugly. "Do you think if I just blurt out all the sordid details it will be as easy as one-two-three? Well, no way. Hell, if that were true, Martin could have helped me. Believe me, after what I've put him through, that would be an accomplishment."

Josh didn't interrupt while Elaine aired out her feelings. He wanted her to get out all the anger.

Josh's silence was a learned science. What Elaine, or for that matter most of his newfound friends, didn't know about him was he held a degree in psychology. He didn't practice medically because his creative ego won the battle.

He had all the intensions of someday picking up where he left off and beginning to practice. But for the time being, he kept his medical degree a secret.

After Elaine settled down, Josh imposed the question he had patiently been waiting to ask. With a combination of concern and passion, Josh finally asked, "Exactly why did you come here tonight?"

Elaine's silence made it obvious to Josh that she was unaware of why she had chosen to be with him. Rarely, if ever, did she take the time to think any situation through. She just forged ahead and did whatever presented itself to her. Right or wrong, that was her.

Impulsively, Elaine asked, "Do you think I can stay here until tomorrow?"

Josh nodded. "Fine by me, but what do you say we call it a night. Let's just get some sleep. It's already after five. What do you say Elaine, rest?"

"You go ahead," Elaine said as she walked over toward the window. "I think I'll just sit here for awhile. If that's okay with you."

Josh neared Elaine. He cautiously kissed her forehead and said, "That's fine. If you need me, you know where I'll be."

At that moment, Elaine and Josh each went their separate ways. As Josh looked back, a smile appeared on his face, as he thought of how wonderful it would be if Elaine raced into his arms and confessed her love.

They would kiss and, like magic, they would be one. Their harmony would be indisputable and filled with passion. Then he turned away, reminding himself that was only a fantasy of his.

Elaine waited until Josh had disappeared from her view before walking toward the massive window, where she could let her imagination take her to places she had never been before. Anywhere but reality.

She stood alone for what seemed like quite a long time, agonizing about what Martin would think about her letter. He would be so disappointed, but maybe he would realize she had been right all along.

In the stillness of the early morning hours, Elaine paced the floor of Josh's apartment. She felt comfortable enough to pick up and hold several of Josh's ornaments. Just from touching them, Elaine could feel the sentiment behind several of his artifacts.

Josh was not the man he appeared to be. He had a rather gentle, boyish side to him. Someday, she thought, he would find the right woman. A woman who could make him as happy as he should be. Unfortunately, she was not that woman, and never could be.

Standing there watching the quietness of life, Elaine had uncovered several things about herself that she had neatly tucked away for years in the inner folds of her own secret world. Now that they were opened, she wished she had left well enough alone.

Out of all this sadness filtering through her body, a brief smile came to her face as she thought of Mac. If she had met Mac years earlier, maybe they could have helped each other. She disagreed with the theory it was never too late.

Mac was very different from Josh or Martin. Maybe it was Vietnam and the loneliness of his heart that attracted her. She had never before been so overpowered by anyone. Remembering their brief time together panicked her.

She was sleepy but fought it, certain if she went to bed she would once again have those horrible nightmares.

In the morning, Josh tiptoed out of his bedroom and stood by the door, watching Elaine. At first she didn't realize he was there, but when she did she was startled. "I thought you'd be sleeping for hours. What happened?"

"I guess I wasn't as tired as I thought. I'm on my way into the kitchen. I'm starved. Will you join me?"

"In a minute or two," she promised.

Josh nodded and said, "You'd better hurry. I should warn you. When I get hungry, I really get hungry. There's no telling what the hell I'll eat."

Just as Josh was about to eat his third peanut butter and banana sandwich, Elaine came into the kitchen, sat down in the chair across from him and asked, "Do you ever feel lonely?"

"Sometimes, but it passes. I'll tell you one thing — I like having you here with me. I know this whole thing about you and me might be wrong, but I'm very satisfied eating my peanut butter while I'm looking at you."

The faint blush appearing on Elaine's face gave reason for another confession from Josh. "That's the other reason. Your innocence, it's charming. I don't know any other woman quite like you."

Elaine's mood reversed drastically and her tone of voice changed as a cold, unhappy look appeared on her face. "Boy, have you got me wrong. Innocent? No, I don't think so. If anything, impure might describe me. Maybe even contemptible, but not innocent. I think you've got the wrong woman."

"Why are you so dammed hard on yourself?" Josh asked, trying his level-headed best to understand her.

"You think I'm too hard on myself?" she asked. "I think you've got it all wrong. I'm not hard enough."

Josh tried to change the subject, but it was too late. Elaine was already far too upset.

Josh thought for a moment before he spoke. "Okay, I've got it. Is there anything you really enjoy?"

"No, not really," Elaine answered.

"There must be something that interests you," Josh insisted. "We'll do it. Whatever it is, we'll do it. Then you'll feel better. I'm sure of that. So tell me, what is it you like?"

"I like the symphony," Elaine relinquished her favored passion to Josh. "But I'm not going to the symphony right now. I don't know where I'm going, but I'm going. I think I've outstayed my welcome."

"Hold on, no one's going anywhere. I'm sorry. It's just that I wanted to make you feel better. It's my fault. I won't bring this up again," Josh explained. "Why don't you come with me? I'll put you up in my guest room. I promise not to bother you in any way. You need some rest more than you need anything else."

When Elaine stood up, the room began to spin. "Oh my," she said. "Maybe you're right, I do need some sleep."

From the moment Elaine's head touched the pillow, she fell fast asleep.

Chapter 12

Martin came home earlier than expected. While riding home, he assured himself that he would make things right between Elaine and himself. He would do whatever it took. He was determined not to live the rest of his life in limbo.

Much to his surprise, he felt a sudden sense of loss when he walked into the house. There was complete quiet and an eeriness that existed among the walls.

"Elaine, are you here?" he called out as he walked up the stairs and into their bedroom. "Maggie, what about you? Are you home?"

When he realized he was alone, he undressed and walked right into the shower, not noticing the letter addressed to him that lay peacefully on his bed.

As he showered, his mind wandered to thoughts of Iris and Becky. They had been so very happy. It was too perfect. A man and woman who never went to bed angry. They could talk to each other about anything. No secrets, no lies, just love.

Each night at dinner, they aired their differences, if they had any. Many nights passed without a grievance, only laughter and conversation — especially as they watched their daughter grow.

He loved Iris as he now loved Elaine. The difference was, Iris loved him back.

Loving Elaine and sheltering her had begun to become impossible. He knew if they had any chance at all, honesty and real hard work were the only things that could keep them together.

Once again, Martin ran the water over his face, trying to wash away the tears. After his shower, he fell back against the bed for what seemed like a very long time, but wasn't.

When he awoke, he noticed the letter. He quickly opened it, terrified of its contents.

He could hear Elaine's voice echoing in his ears as he read on.

Dear Martin:

I don't know if you'll understand what I'm about to say, but maybe in time you'll find it in your heart to forgive my selfishness. There hasn't been one day since Stevie was born that I haven't loved him. I even loved Stevie before he was born. So as you are now finding out, I really did love my son, but what good is love that has conditions? The only real love is unconditional. That is the only love you know.

Goodbye Martin. I love you and I love Stevie.

Elaine

Just then, Martin heard someone come into the house. He called out, "Elaine, is that you?"

"No, it 's me, Doctor," Maggie answered as she put down the bag of groceries she was carrying. "You're back early."

Martin continued walking down the stairs as he spoke. "I thought it would be better if I didn't leave Elaine alone too long, but I guess I was too late. When did she leave?"

Maggie shrugged her shoulders. "I don't really know. When I knocked on your bedroom door with a breakfast tray for her, she was gone. All I saw was a letter addressed to you."

Martin sat down, still holding the letter to his chest. His sense of loss depressed him. His voice faded into low volume. "She's left me. It's all in this letter."

Maggie's tone was harsh. "What do you mean she's left you? It just isn't possible."

" I'm afraid it's true," Martin said as he suddenly became aware of the horrifying truth. "Oh my God, she's left me. What the hell do I do now? I've lost again."

Now was not the time to keep secrets from Maggie. He handed her the letter from Elaine and watched her as she read on.

"Oh my God, Martin. I'm so sorry."

Martin's mood veered to extreme frustration. "Damn it, I don't even know what to do. I can't believe that it's come this far. I should have seen it coming. Maybe she'll change her mind. She'll come back. I know she will."

"I think we should call the police," Maggie suggested.

"No, I can't do that," Martin said, his voice filled with anticipation. "Not yet. Maybe she'll call and I can convince her to come home. Something's got to happen that will change this mess around."

Still sitting on the step, Martin placed his hands on his knees and, in one awkward move, lowered his head. "Elaine," he whispered, "Please come home."

Martin grew impatient but still refused to call the police. Finally, after several hours, Maggie convinced him to call Sally Braverman. What Martin needed now was a good friend, and Sally was just that.

Not wasting any time, Sally appeared on Martin's doorstep looking as glamorous as ever.

Maggie smiled as she opened the door, but before she could get a word in, Sally asked, "So how is he?"

Maggie's face clouded with tension. "I don't know. I finally got him to rest. Shall I wake him?"

"No," Sally said as she followed Maggie into the kitchen. "He needs his rest. I only hope this isn't too much for him."

Maggie and Sally sipped coffee and reminded each other of how severely Elaine's disappearance would hurt Martin.

"Damn it, I hope she calls," Sally said as she doused her umpteenth cigarette. "I really hope Martin can handle this. Sometimes it's even too hard for a person like Martin to accept failure. I just pray Martin can handle this whole awful mess."

"Me too," Maggie said in agreement.

Neither of them noticed Martin standing at the kitchen doorway. "In answer to your question, this is not too much for me. It can't be. Elaine is my wife and I want her back. Don't worry, I'll be fine. It's Elaine who I'm worried about."

Martin had always put himself last, and Elaine's leaving would once again jeopardize his life.

He worried. Sally and Maggie watched, observing devastation at its root. Once more, they waited to mold the pieces back together should Martin's world repeat itself and explode.

Privately, Sally's thoughts turned to Josh. Before arriving at Martin's, she had made a phone call to his gallery. She had hoped to reach him before he could talk Elaine into doing something stupid. After all, she wouldn't have been the first.

But Josh was supposedly away on business. Some business, Sally thought. Another imprint on his bed, another regret. Poor Elaine, another fool.

For a long while, there wasn't much conversation between the three of them. Maggie made the coffee, and they all drank it. They waited quietly for the telephone to ring.

Delaying the inevitable was certainly too damn hard. Sally grew tired of watching Martin's sadness cultivate something much worse, depression. Damn it, Sally thought, why did life have to be so fucking hard?

Martin and Sally's friendship went back more than thirty years. They lived on the same block in the old neighborhood. It was a time when money meant something and having none was the norm.

They both went to Hibbard Grade School. That was so long ago, but Sally often reminded herself of the dime store they used to walk by every day on their way to school, long before either of them had even an extra fifty cents in their pocket.

She would want to stop for her usual piece of licorice and a gumball, but Martin would want to go straight home. He had promised his mother he wouldn't spoil his appetite for dinner. Even then, for one harmless piece of licorice and a gumball, Martin wouldn't disobey his mother.

So he waited patiently outside for Sally. Sometimes she gave him the red gumball, his favorite, which he always promised to eat after dinner. Even then, he was exacting.

Sally's memory still recalled that little, chubby boy who struggled so hard to make his life right. He swept floors and cleaned toilets, anything to put some change in his pockets.

She had never even told Martin that she had seen him cry the night his father died. It was a fast, low-pain death. First there was that sharp, intruding pain, then the dizziness. In what amounted to minutes, it was over. Max Lewis was dead.

Sally had always liked and respected Max. He was a righteous man who, for whatever reason, always helped his friends. Especially Sally. That she would never forget.

At sixteen, she had met a boy who thought he was a man. He was nineteen. Sally was a girl who thought she could be a woman. They were both children, too young to have a child of their own, but old enough to make a baby.

Sally turned to Max for help. He gave her money to have an abortion. He didn't approve, but he still helped. "Obligation , life is filled with obligations," he would say. "A real man does the right thing."

Max kept her secret from everyone, including Martin. In return, Sally promised herself no matter what happened in life, she would always be there for Martin.

Martin was a part of Max and for Sally, he was a way of holding on to the past. Just as Sally knew Max would never disappoint her, she knew he had raised a son with the highest of principles. Martin was, and would always be, as fine a man as his father.

Max would say, "Martin, you will be the doctor I couldn't be. You will show the world that Max Lewis did something right. He had a son, a wonderful son. A doctor, no less."

Chapter 13

That night at Sophie's house, Stevie was the last child tucked into bed. As Sophie sat by his side, she lovingly stroked his forehead and whispered softly into his ear, "Goodnight sweetie, I love you."

Stevie smiled innocently as he gave Sophie the tightest bear hug he could. "Good night, Mommy, goodnight."

Sophie adored that one word, mommy. Stevie always reminded her of her own little boy, Robbie. That was the reason why when Stevie referred to her as mommy, she didn't discourage him. It only seemed to happen when he was really tired or really upset. It didn't seem to hurt anyone, so she let it go.

Sometimes Sophie got mad at herself for having a favorite child. She knew it was wrong, but some things couldn't be helped. Stevie was so good, and what a heart of gold he had. He shared with the other children so unselfishly. Over the years, Sophie had begun to believe Stevie had truly been born with a special gift.

Along the road there had been many children, but Stevie had always felt like her own flesh and blood. Their relationship had clicked into place right from the start.

Stevie had been asleep for hours when Sophie heard loud whimpering and then a horrifying scream. "Mommy, Mommy, no! Don't!"

Nervously woken by Stevie's scream, Sophie could feel her heart beating faster and faster. Her heart immediately quieted down as soon as she peeked into his room and saw that he was sound asleep.

"You're fine," Sophie whispered as she sat on the edge of his bed, watching him sleep, making certain he was alright. She remained at his bedside for quite a long time. As always, she would be there if he needed her.

***

At approximately the same time Stevie bellowed out, it occurred to Josh that Elaine had been very quiet.

Ten minutes prior, Josh had been talking to Elaine through the bathroom door. He couldn't hear her answers because of the intensity of the shower water beating against the glass door. Conversation was difficult, but Josh specialized in non-stop talk, sometimes to a fault.

When he realized the shower water had stopped, he immediately doused his cigarette and pulled on his pants. At the same time, he called out to Elaine, "Are you alright? You're awfully quiet. Elaine, talk to me."

Josh was becoming slightly uneasy, trying not to panic. "Elaine, please don't do this. Tell me you're alright. Come on, hon, please. Elaine, what's going on in there?"

There was a sudden silence in the apartment. Josh didn't speak. The air seemed stale. There was no movement in the bedroom and not a single sound coming from the bathroom. Josh took a deep breath, certain something had happened.

One more time, Josh called out in a somewhat angered tone. "Elaine, this isn't funny. Please say something or I'm coming in. One ... two ... three. That's it, I'm coming in right now."

Those were his last words before pushing the door open. He stood there for a moment, unable to speak. Then, as if lightning shot through him, Josh screamed louder than he had ever thought possible. "Oh my God, Elaine, what did you do? Oh no..."

Elaine was blanketed with bright, red blood.

Josh fell to his knees. Then, sliding toward her, he put his head on her chest and pressed his trembling fingers on her neck, silently praying for a miracle.

With only the slightest fragment of indulgence and the spirit of the moment, his prayers had been answered. There was a faint pulse. Elaine was still alive.

The paramedics came barreling into the room. There were three of them - two women and one man. They immediately raced toward Elaine.

After a quick but thorough look at Elaine, the male paramedic walked back toward the phone and dialed into the hospital emergency system.

The paramedic reported, detail by detail, the events immediately as they were happening. The hospital required exact monitoring of serious conditions. Elaine's suicide attempt qualified.

The male paramedic motioned to Josh and then called out to him, "Why don't you have a seat in the other room? It will be better for all of us. We need access to the room at all times."

Josh nodded, only too happy to be secluded. He had always hated the sight of blood. Several minutes later, the nausea hit him.

Josh, still shaky from this entire mess, quickly went into the kitchen and pulled out several pieces of ice from the refrigerator. He sucked the ice cubes with extreme intensity, and the nausea started to disappear.

The memory of an old football injury came to his mind. Seventy stitches in his arm and a complete leg cast accounted for his anxiety.

Deep breaths helped, but despite all these memories, he found himself answering yes when the paramedics asked if he would go with Elaine to the hospital.

At the hospital, Elaine and the paramedics were met by a team of doctors and nurses. They worked on her for what seemed like a long time, but in actuality had been only minutes.

They finally acknowledged Josh's presence. After being told that Elaine would live, he seemed to be in the way. So, without saying goodbye, Josh walked away, unsure of what to do.

Halfway down the hall, it occurred to him that even though Elaine had showed her disappointment in life and her marriage, there were two sides to every story. Her husband needed to know.

Josh pulled a handful of change from his pocket. Without really knowing what to say, he dialed Elaine's home.

Martin answered in a rather desperate tone. "Hello."

Upon hearing his voice, Josh paused. The reality began to set in. Elaine did indeed have another life and, most likely, a husband who loved her very much.

Martin repeated, "Hello. Elaine, is that you? Please say something."

Josh knew he had to speak, especially as he listened to Martin's desperation. "It's not Elaine," he said in a rather clumsy way.

"Well then, who are you?" Martin asked in a serious tone.

"It doesn't matter who I am. All that matters is Elaine needs you."

Martin didn't understand. "What do you mean Elaine needs me? What's going on? What's happened to her?"

Sally, who had been in the adjoining room, quickly jumped up when she heard Martin's frantic tone.

For the first time in Josh's very verbal life, he couldn't seem to speak. He stood there eyeing the phone, deciding if he should hang up or go on. Realizing there really was no choice, he shouted into the phone, "Elaine has tried to commit suicide."

Martin's face turned white. "Oh my God. Oh no."

Sally immediately stood next to Martin. She placed her hand on his shoulder, acknowledging her support for whatever had just happened. Obviously, the news was not good.

Martin took a moment to catch his breath. Then he asked, "Where are you calling from?"

"The Meridian," Josh replied, thinking to himself exactly how hard a call like this was to receive. But not to forget, it was equally hard to make. In the light of this matter, they were equal.

Martin's trembling voice proceeded to question him. "Is she alive?"

"Yes, she is," Josh replied, getting ready to hang up.

"Please tell me who you are," Martin pleaded.

"It's not necessary. All that matters now is your wife needs you. Go to her."

Those were Josh's last words as he hung up the phone and headed down the hall.

***

Martin raced into the hospital with Sally close behind. He was shaking, but remained refined as he spoke to the nursing staff in the emergency room.

Martin noticed a longtime friend of his who was seated behind the information desk. Trying not to be frantic, Martin asked, "Do you know where Elaine is? I received a call telling me she was here."

The woman behind the desk responded quickly. "Yes, Martin, she's here."

"Where is she? I want to see her."

The woman from behind the desk stood up and walked around to where Martin was standing, directing him to have a seat. "I'll page her, Doctor," she said, making sure Martin was comfortable.

Inwardly, Martin wanted to shout out, "What the hell is going on here? Don't treat me like everyone else. My wife is in there and I'm scared. Tell me what's going on. I'm on staff here, I'm not like everyone else. Don't patronize me."

But he didn't say that. In fact, he didn't say a word until he saw Valerie walking toward him.

Martin stood up. "Valerie, what are you doing here?" he asked, stunned by her presence.

In a quick but concerned fashion, Valerie answered. "I'm Elaine's doctor."

"Since when?" Martin asked, bewildered by this entire situation. He waited impatiently for an answer.

Valerie paused for a moment. "Not very long. I was hoping it would never get to this. I wanted Elaine to talk with you. If she had, maybe this horrible nightmare wouldn't have happened. But you'll have to excuse me. I have to check on Elaine and then we'll talk."

Martin reached out and grasped Valerie's arm. "Val, please tell me what's going on. I want to see Elaine."

"In a little while, but not now. I don't think it would be a good idea."

Contrary to Martin's usual behavior, he raised his voice. Heads turned as he spoke. "My wife is in there. I want to know what happened. Now."

Valerie didn't lose her cool. She never did. "Look Martin, you're a wonderful doctor and I know you've probably been in this very same position many times, but for right now you're going to have to understand. Elaine is my patient and she comes first. Isn't that exactly what you would do?"

"Yes but..."

Valerie interrupted. "Then please let me do my job," Valerie added as she patted Martin's shoulder in a consoling manner. "I'll be back shortly."

Before Valerie got a chance to walk away, Martin held her back as he grasped her arm. "Please Val, just tell me. Is she going to live?"

Valerie answered with optimism. "Yes, I think so."

That was all Martin needed to hear. He walked back toward Sally who, even after reading the no-smoking sign, had lit up a cigarette anyway.

"Want one?" she asked as she offered the pack to Martin.

"We haven't smoked in years."

Sally responded quickly. "Maybe you haven't. But whenever I'm nervous, I take one. Sometimes it's more than just one. Tonight it's probably going to be an entire pack."

Martin sat down and nervously tapped the table with his fingers. "I don't think a cigarette is what I need. I need to see Elaine right now."

Martin stood up, just about to violate Valerie's decision, when Sally took hold of his arm. "Martin, please sit down. I'm sure Elaine's doctor and the staff are doing everything they should be."

"Sal, do you know what kind of doctor Valerie Mitchell is?" he asked, certain she didn't.

"No, why?"

"She's a gynecologist."

Sally was near speechless. All she could say was, "Oh."

However, Martin did take heed of what Sally had said and sat down. He wondered why on earth Elaine hadn't come to him. Then the realization set in. She couldn't trust him.

He had once again failed his wife. He began to question if there really was a God. He wondered why he had been chosen to lose his love again.

Martin and Sally had minimal conversation in the waiting room, neither seeming to have the energy. Martin did take Sally up on her offer. He lit a cigarette, but put it out after several pointless drags. Nothing could obstruct his agony.

When Valerie Mitchell approached, he stood up. Not only were his hands a bit unsteady, but his eyes seemed to have lost focus. He was running on empty.

Valerie seemed to understand. Looking more satisfied than before, she spoke in a slightly more relaxed tone. "Things are definitely looking up. Physically, there's improvement and I think we're more than halfway out of the woods."

Sally smiled as she stood up and embraced Martin. She whispered in his ear, "I knew it all along. God watches over."

"Val, can I see her now?"

"Yes, but only after we speak. Can we talk in private?" Valerie asked. "I would like to tell you exactly what happened."

"It's okay. We can talk out here. Sally's like family," Martin said in an anxious tone.

Valerie nodded. "I'm sure she is, but I would prefer our conversation be held in private."

Martin responded to Sally's hand motioning him to go with the doctor. "Are you okay on that?" he asked, not wanting to offend her.

"I'll wait for you here," was Sally's considerate reply. "Don't worry, hon, I'll be fine. Go."

Martin followed Valerie into a private office where she closed the door. "Martin, have a seat."

Martin would rather have stood, but he did as she asked. "How bad is it?" was his first question.

"It will depend on your definition of bad. The reason I've been seeing Elaine was because she was pregnant."

Valerie paused for a moment when she realized she had caught him totally by surprise. Martin closed his eyes for a moment, trying to comprehend exactly what Valerie had just said.

First he responded as a doctor. "I know what's next. She lost the baby, didn't she?" He didn't have to wait for a response. He had also been on the other side.

Then Martin responded as the angered husband and the father of the unborn would. He awkwardly cleared his throat. "Why the hell did she do this? I wish she would have let me help her. Damn it, this didn't have to happen."

Valerie nodded in agreement. "No, it didn't. But it happened, there's no denying that. What you have to do is go on from here."

"It's going to be hard, more than a little hard," Martin confessed.

"If it's any consolation, I agree with you, but my hands were tied," Valerie confessed. "I wanted Elaine to discuss her pregnancy with you, but she wouldn't. I agonized about invading what had been a private matter. As you well know, Elaine was my patient and I did as she asked."

"I know that," Martin admitted. "So, where do we go from here? What's our next step?"

"Well, I must be frank about all of this. Your wife really hates herself. Whatever her reasons are, she's created an entire wall around her."

"I know," Martin agreed as he went on to explain further. "Her life before we met had been filled with lots of regrets and bad feelings. I often asked her to get some help. I was willing to do whatever it took."

"Martin, I think she needs a little bit more than just some help. She sliced herself pretty bad. It's lucky she's still alive. If she hadn't been brought in when she had, she would have bled to death. And then we wouldn't have been given this chance to help her. I'll tell you, God was watching over her."

"Do you know who brought her in?" Martin reluctantly asked.

"He didn't give a name."

"Well, that doesn't really matter anyway," Martin admitted. "What really matters is we get Elaine the help she needs. Did she happen to tell you about our son Stevie?"

"Yes, but in a roundabout way. She's been crying out Stevie's name all night. I just hadn't put the pieces together. That is, until you called him by name."

Martin drew a long, deep breath. "I don't know what to say about our life together. I love her so damn much, but she keeps so much inside of her. It doesn't leave much room for anyone else. Maybe this is all my fault."

Valerie's tone changed. "Absolutely not. You can't blame yourself. Your love isn't enough, no one could have helped Elaine. She's got to be willing to face the truth about herself."

"And just how do we get her to do that?"

A slight pause occurred before Valerie released her opinion. "Martin, Elaine needs extensive help. She needs Ben Caufield."

Martin was taken by surprise at Valerie's suggestion. "Ben Caufield? The Castleberry Pavilion?"

"Elaine needs to do this alone, away from all pressures that would hold her back. She needs the kind of therapy only Ben can give."

"Am I a pressure because I love her?" Martin asked, really wanting to understand Valerie's conclusion.

"In this situation, as in so many others, love isn't always enough."

"She'll never agree," Martin assured her.

"She already has," Valerie conceded.

Martin's eyes expressed surprise. "Well, I guess what they say about you is true."

"And that is?" Valerie questioned.

"They say you don't take no for an answer. Now I understand just what that meant," Martin added.

Before leaving, Valerie stood up and reached for Martin's hand. She held onto it and said, "If I see a family worth fighting for, you'd better believe I'm going to fight."

"Is that what you see us as, a family worth fighting for?" Martin asked with interest.

Valerie smiled with finality. "Absolutely."

***

Morning came and went. Martin returned home from the hospital two days later, never sleeping a wink. When he was satisfied Elaine was going to be fine, he said his thank yous to the nursing staff, waved goodbye and left.

Maggie knocked before entering Martin's room. "I think you might need this," she said as she placed a cup of coffee and a muffin on the table beside him.

"Thanks," Martin said as he immediately reached over toward the coffee. "You're right. This is just what the doctor ordered."

Martin gazed over at the clock. "Oh no. I didn't call Stevie yesterday," Martin said as he picked up the phone to dial.

Sophie answered in her usual, friendly tone.

"Hello Sophie, it's Martin Lewis."

"Oh, thank goodness it's you. I was a little alarmed, thinking something terrible had happened. A day without a call from you is highly unusual. I was just about to call your office."

"I'm sorry, Sophie, really I am. The last few days weren't exactly my best."

"Is everything okay now?" Sophie asked with concern.

"Yes, I think everything is going to be just fine," Martin said sincerely.

"Good," Sophie replied. "Stevie misses you."

"Is he doing alright?" Martin asked with worry.

"He's fine. I kept him very busy so he wouldn't notice you hadn't called."

"Can I talk to him?" Martin asked.

"Of course," Sophie said, smoothing out Stevie's hair. "He just walked into the room and he's standing here beside me." Sophie handed the phone to Stevie.

"How's my boy?" Martin eagerly asked.

Stevie smiled into the phone. "Daddy, Daddy. Ice cream, ice cream."

"Tomorrow we will have all the ice cream you can possibly eat. Love you."

"Bye," Stevie said as his eyes focused on the pizza sitting on the table.

Sophie took hold of the phone. "Everything's under control at this end. It's Danny's birthday and I ordered a pizza for lunch. You know what that means."

"Yep, party time. Have fun. See you tomorrow," Martin said as he hung up the phone, wishing he were there.

Chapter 14

Several months later, in the dead of winter, Elaine sat quietly in her room at the Castleberry Pavilion, watching the snow fall.

"Come in," Elaine said with a whisper after the second knock.

A tall, rather large woman approached Elaine. "Hello dear, how do you feel today?" she asked with utmost compassion and sincerity. This woman was the head nurse at the Castleberry for more than ten years and probably would be for at least ten more.

She had once been known as Sister Mary Lynne, but that was a very long time ago. Now she was just plain old Mary, and that's the way she liked it.

Mary's patients were her friends. Under different conditions, she might have had an outside life. Maybe it was her own inadequacies or maybe she just wasn't suitable for the world she chose. She was a little between both worlds, not exactly fitting into either. Mary was a wonderful nurse. At the Castleberry, that was all that mattered.

Elaine shrugged her shoulders and responded unassumingly. "I feel horrible and very sad. I don't know, today seems like such a long day. I just feel like going to sleep. I hate it when it snows."

Mary reached for her hand and helped her up. "Come on dear, Dr. Caufield has arranged some extra time for you."

Elaine pulled the back down on her chair. "I really don't feel like talking today, maybe tomorrow. I'm too tired to talk."

"I'm afraid you can't just stay in your room. It's been three days since you've talked with the doctor. It will do you good. I'll walk you down," Mary said as she helped Elaine push herself up. This time Elaine grabbed hold of Mary's hand. Elaine held on a lot tighter than usual.

The sign on the door read, "Dr. Benjamin Caufield." Elaine looked toward Mary and asked, "Do you think you could come in with me? Just today, please?"

Mary sympathized, but shook her head. "You know I can't do that. It's better if you and the doctor are alone. You know Dr. Caufield's a good man. He wants to help you. Let him," Mary said in a reassuring way.

She felt Elaine's hand immediately slip away. "Good girl," Mary said as she gave Elaine a hug. "It's going to be okay. You'll see."

Mary waited outside the office, just until she could sense Elaine had made herself somewhat comfortable. Walking down the hall, Mary looked up and silently prayed, reaching for her cross. She held onto it, reminding herself Elaine had a long way to go.

"Dear God," she prayed. "Give Elaine the strength she needs to get better, even a small improvement would be appreciated. Please God, she's a fine young woman. She needs a second chance. Please give it to her. Thank you," she murmured as she continued walking down the hall.

Ben Caufield was quite an impressive-looking man. He had dark, black hair, slightly graying at the temples. He had a kind smile and a soothing voice. But when Elaine looked at him eye-to-eye, she felt uneasy.

Regardless of how Ben Caufield came across to others, to Elaine he represented confronting her past, and that made her uncomfortable.

"Is today a better day for you?" Ben asked, certain Elaine's response would be the same.

"No. Now can I go back to my room?" Elaine asked in a hopeful manner.

"In a little while," Ben promised as he sat in silence, hoping Elaine would finally break the ice and speak to him.

As usual, the conversation remained a stalemate.

Their visit came to a halt when there was a knock at the door. Ben stood up and walked toward the door. He wasn't surprised to see Mary.

Mary smiled in a thoughtful way. "If you'll excuse me for interrupting, Doctor, I would be grateful. We have a problem."

Ben shook his head as he closed the door behind him, leaving Elaine for a moment. "Well my dear Mary Lynn, who needs me more?" Mary didn't seem to mind when Ben called her Mary Lynn. That name was restricted just for his use and he knew that.

Mary's eyes held that deep, hurry-please stare that Ben understood. Mary had always felt safe at the Castleberry and with Ben Caufield. He was a real take-charge kind of guy, and Mary admired him for that.

Mary's voice held a bit of panic. "Jessie's pretty bad today. She refuses to get out of the bathtub."

Ben walked back into his office toward where Elaine was seated. "Elaine," he asked, "Shall we wrap it up for today, or would you like to wait in here for me? I have some business to attend to."

Elaine just sat there with a horrible, blank expression on her face. Ben had become accustomed to her ways, so this didn't phase him in the least.

Elaine had no intention of their session going anywhere today or, for that matter, any other day. Regardless of how long she sat in the hot seat, her lips were sealed.

***

Another month had passed. Elaine still refused to converse with Ben Caufield about any subject other than customary parting dialogue. In fact, she sometimes fell asleep during her therapy sessions.

That didn't seem to stop Ben from continuing on with her sessions. Occasionally, an emotional sentiment came from her eyes, a sentiment Ben would get back to at a later date. Somehow it all worked to his benefit, regardless of how difficult the patient was. To Ben, each patient was as important as the next.

One day it would happen for Elaine. With a little bit of luck and some leverage, Ben would be able to break into her system. Ben wasn't likely to give up on anybody. Over the years, he had come to believe that waiting was important. Timing was everything.

Sometimes he compared his job to that of a cat burglar. The mind took a little more prodding, but there was usually a way in.

Finally, it occurred to Ben that he had been going at this all wrong. He had a patient as stubborn as Elaine once before.

It was a long time ago, but he remembered. Her name was Sister Mary Lynn. He focused back to those dark, brown eyes that were in so much pain.

It wasn't until he forced the situation that Mary Lynn opened up her heart and let the anger separate. Mary Lynn had come to him on a referral. She had been a nun for many years and was on the verge of giving up her vows. She was in love with a wonderful man and was about to make a change.

Night after night, Mary Lynn was in torment. Her restlessness never stopped. She hadn't told a soul about Richard or any of her dreams. Finally, the decision had been made. She was going to leave the convent and marry Richard.

Everything almost turned out remarkably well. It was to be a surprise. In fact, she hadn't even told Richard of her choice.

Mary Lynn was in love. To delay her marriage would have been ludicrous. She wanted to build a new life and leaving the church was the only path she could have taken.

Never before had Mary been so expeditious. She usually took her time and plotted out the course of action best suited for her. But not that time. She was in quite a hurry to have a life. Then, without even a warning, everything changed.

It all happened fast. Her beloved Richard was killed in a plane crash. She was too late and so was their love.

At that time, Ben was rather new at the game. He was tough enough, but he questioned if he was good enough. Mary had a strong will and an empty heart. That combination was rough.

Ben did succeed in winning Mary Lynn over, but not until he compromised his training. He would do the same with Elaine. It was time. He needed the challenge. There came a time when even the best of doctors needed to push just a little bit harder in order to learn.

Elaine sat with her legs curled under her. She was staring outside the window, not expecting what was to follow.

Ben stood beside Elaine and shouted. "You are one hell of a mother. If you're staring out that window hoping for a miracle, there won't be one. When you wake up in the morning, you will still have a son but, guess what, he doesn't have a mother. Not exactly a facsimile of the perfect mother. You are one mean bitch. Shall I go on?" he asked. "Because there's plenty more I think you might need to know about yourself."

It didn't take more than a second or two until Elaine stood up and screamed at the top of her lungs. "Just who the hell do you think you are to call me a bitch? You don't know me at all. I thought you were supposed to be a doctor."

"I am a doctor. And believe it or not, even doctors get tired of this bullshit. This sorry-for-yourself attitude isn't going to do one damn thing for you. You want to know something my dear, you're absolutely right about one thing. I don't know you, and at this rate I never will."

Now they could begin. Ben Caufield had accomplished his mission. However, Elaine's words didn't come easily. Ben had to work for them.

At first Elaine spoke only of what she had been feeling that day. Then they progressed to a possible yesterday and maybe even several days that had passed. Elaine's childhood memories were still unspoken.

Martin had called Ben every day, impatiently waiting for a visit with Elaine. He wouldn't even ask a question or appear inquisitive in any way concerning her recovery. Five minutes would do just fine, but the waiting was impossible.

It was Sunday and Martin had just come home from visiting Stevie. He had been depleted of all his resourcefulness and cheerful conversational skills. He had slowly been growing tired of his life or lack of it. In other words, he was starting to feel sorry for himself.

It hadn't happened overnight. In fact, he wasn't even certain when it happened.

Sunday was family night, and again he was alone. The house was quiet, too quiet. The walls were filled with lonely silence and unhappy thoughts.

He stared at the TV dinner he had just prepared. It didn't look quite as appetizing as a good plate of pasta from Angelo's, but he ate it anyway. What he needed was a friend to talk to, but his options weren't very clear.

Maggie was visiting her aunt, while Sally had booked herself on what she called a love cruise. Cecil, who had finally made time to travel, flew to Europe. Then there was his mother, Esther, who had decided there was more to life than an occasional bridge game. She left for Florida weeks ago.

After dinner, Martin sat down in his usual chair. He reached for the remote and turned on the TV. He had even tired of television. Nothing seemed to fill his empty hours.

He was now well into his forties, rapidly approaching fifty. Even with all the friends and colleagues he had acquired over the years, he still felt alone. He missed Elaine and what could have been their life.

Martin reached into his pocket and pulled out his car keys. He was going to visit Elaine at the Castleberry Pavilion. The hell with waiting. Time wasn't healing his wounds.

Once on the expressway, Martin assured himself he was doing the right thing. He was just about to cross the state line, seconds away from Wisconsin and only hours away from Elaine, when he realized he was about to make a mistake.

He had only been thinking of himself. When Elaine was ready to see him, Ben would let him know. A surprise visit might not be in her best interest. At the next ramp, Martin turned off and headed back home.

Later that night, Martin was awoken by loud, crashing thunder. When he noticed he had fallen asleep completely dressed, he removed his shoes first. He had been so very tired that sleeping with his clothes on seemed quite ordinary for him.

Suddenly, a bolt of flashing current sped through the house. The electricity was out. Martin reached over to Elaine's nightstand for the flashlight, but instead he pulled out a small diary. It was dark, but he was certain what he had in his hands was indeed a diary. There was an opening for a key. However, it wasn't locked.

Again Martin reached toward the back of the nightstand and pulled out a flashlight. It was just bright enough to read with. Guilt had occurred to him, but he still opened the diary and read on.

***

Jan .3

To my dearest diary
My friend, my only friend

It happened on January 1. My baby was born. My Stevie was born all wrong. It wasn't supposed to be this way. I don't care what the doctors say, it is my fault. This is my baby. God, please fix my baby. All my dreams are gone. What am I supposed to do? Why did you do this to me? What did I do wrong? I know, it's because of my sister, isn't it? It's because I was responsible for Megan's death. You're punishing me. Yes, that's it. My punishment is my son.

Elaine

Jan. 5

To my dearest diary
My friend, my only friend

I held Stevie today. He smelled so good, so fresh, so unafraid of the world that would never accept him. It felt so right holding him. It was just as if he belonged in my arms. When I kissed his forehead, I felt the softness of his skin. He didn't cry when I held him. Do you think he knew that I was his mother? I hope not. He might hate me. He should hate me. I hate me.

Elaine

Martin wiped the tears from his eyes. He felt a closeness to Elaine that he had never felt before. He thought for a moment, before continuing, of how he might have been able to help her. Of course, that would have been true only if she had let him.

Jan. 7

To my dearest diary
My friend, my only friend
    Stevie's gone. He's gone from my life. He's gone forever. The woman in the long, black coat took my baby while I watched. Look what I've done. I'm Stevie's mother. Why did I let this horrible thing happen? I wish I were dead. I made my baby all wrong. He's not ever going to be like everyone else and it's my fault. My fault.

Elaine

March 19

To my dearest diary
My friend, my only friend
    I haven't written to you for awhile. I haven't been feeling very well. I really don't want to talk to anyone, even Martin. I wish I could open my heart to Martin, but I don't know how. He's such a good man. And who better to know the truth about me. I have no right to ask this of God, but I want my baby back. I want him to be perfect like other babies. You are the only one who knows I love him. I told everyone he died. Poor Martin, look what I've done to him. I made him live a lie. I should be punished. I am punished. I'm alive.

Elaine

***

Martin stopped reading. He couldn't read another word. It was all too horrible. Suddenly he felt inadequate. Had he contributed to the destruction of Elaine's life without realizing it? For hours, Martin agonized over that question before falling off to sleep.

Chapter 15

In the morning and in the light of day, Martin sat sipping his coffee, wondering why he had pretended to have a normal life for the last six years.

He had not understood the pain Elaine felt. Was it his fault for pretending that their problems would somehow disappear? Maybe he should have been the one to get help. After all, he went along with everything Elaine had asked for.

When the telephone rang, Martin felt relieved. He could stop thinking for a moment about Elaine. His mind was on overload.

"Hello," he said as he held the phone to his ear.

"Dr. Lewis," the voice on the other end said. "It's Sarah Winchester. My water just broke."

"Other than that, are you feeling okay?" Martin asked.

"Yes, Doctor. I'm fine," was her reply.

"Good. Then I'll meet you at the hospital."

"Thank you, Doctor. We'll all be there," she said with both promise and excitement in her voice.

After alerting the hospital of Mrs. Winchester's arrival, Martin dressed quickly, never wasting time when a baby was on the way.

He smiled as he drove to the hospital, thinking how wonderful bringing a new life into the world really was. He had been fortunate to have found a profession that brought him such joy.

Hours later, Sarah and Daniel Winchester were the proud parents of a healthy, ten-pound baby boy. They had no idea of just how lucky they really were, but Martin certainly did.

***

Weeks later, Martin had been invited to an art gallery showing. Initially he had said no, but after hearing the gallery owner was about to make a huge donation to the rehabilitation center, he changed his mind.

Even though the decision was last-minute, he did not want to attend alone. Sally had just come home the night before from her cruise. Martin was hesitant to ask her to accompany him, but he did. To go alone would be impossible.

He called Sally in the afternoon. "How about doing me a big favor?" Martin asked.

"Such as?" Sally inquired.

"I need a little companionship," he joked.

Sally laughed. "You? I don't believe the Rock of Gibraltar needs much of anything."

"Really I do. There's a benefit tonight for the rehab center."

"No need to say another word," Sally interrupted. "What time?"

"Seven thirty."

"I'll be waiting," Sally said as she quickly hung up the phone. Then she mumbled, "Uh oh, my hair." She quickly glanced into her mirror and, without a second thought, dialed a number. "Hello, this is Sally Braverman and my hair needs some love and attention." She listened and then repeated, "Three o'clock. Fine, I'll be there."

That night Martin was exactly on time, as always. Sally greeted him with a friendly peck on the cheek. "How's Elaine?" she asked as she got in the car. "This afternoon you didn't say a word about her."

"She still refuses to see me," was Martin's answer, accompanied with a sigh of defeat.

Sally knew Martin long enough to be direct and maybe even a bit harsh. "Where's the spirit? Where's the guy who would stop at nothing to get you to smile? Well, what the hell's going on here?"

Martin's response was quick. "My spirit is out the door. My hands are tied and I don't know what to do. There are times when I think everything's going to be okay, but then I stop kidding myself. I'm not sure about anything anymore."

Sally just listened as Martin aired some of his feelings. She thought they were long overdue.

"Ben Caufield is a hell of a doctor. He's helped many people with his therapy which, although not always conventional, seems to work. I just don't know if he can help Elaine or if I can wait that long."

Sally's mouth opened wide. She was in shock. "Are you telling me what I think you're telling me?"

Martin looked at Sally with a confused look on his face. "What does that mean?"

"It means did you find someone else or are you looking?"

Now it was Martin who was surprised. "You're kidding, aren't you? Another woman? No way. I'm in love with Elaine and I always will be. If she comes home to me, I'll be very grateful. I'm just not sure that she will."

Sally apologetically shrugged her shoulders. "You never know, but I guess I should have. You're a one-woman man. There are so few of you left I almost forgot."

"Now on to the next subject. How was this cruise?" Martin asked with sincerity. "Let's reverse this. Did you find anyone?"

"Yes, I did. Several," Sally boasted in a humorous but humble voice. "Surprised?"

Martin patted Sally's shoulder. "Absolutely not."

Sally talked about her cruise while Martin drove to the fund raiser. For the better part of the ride, Martin continually reminded himself of how alone he really felt. Missing Elaine had become his way of life.

Martin interrupted Sally. "Before we get to the gallery, there's something I have to say. I know what you're trying to do, and I thank you for it."

"What's this all about?" Sally questioned.

"It's about trying your damnedest to help a friend forget his troubles."

"That's what you're paying me for, isn't it?" she joked. "And, by the way, where are we going? You never mentioned where this gala event is."

"It's somewhere on Wells," Martin answered, glancing at the paper he had written the address on. "A man named Derman is the owner. Josh Derman."

Sally's shock kept her silent.

"Anything wrong?" Martin asked, wondering what he had said to cause Sally to react that way.

"Nothing. Nothing at all," Sally answered as she stared out the window, thankful they had just pulled up in front of the gallery. As Martin got out of the car and the parking attendant got in, Sally took a long, deep breath.

Telling Martin about Elaine's small indiscretion would be of no consequence to either. Some things were better left unsaid.

By the time Sally and Martin entered the gallery, champagne toasts and appetizers were being carted around by elegantly tuxedoed waiters and waitresses. The gallery looked magnificent and, for that matter, so did Josh.

Guests were milling around. Some were laughing, some bullshitting and then there were the others trying to find their appropriate category.

When Sally safely assumed Martin had become engaged in a lengthy conversation, she excused herself. At that time she had assured herself Josh hadn't noticed their arrival, a definite plus.

In her usual, fashionable way, Sally nonchalantly walked behind Josh and whispered, "Nice party, asshole." Then she smiled pleasantly.

Josh smiled back at Sally and then whispered in her ear, "You're not still mad at me are you?"

"You mean losing you as a fuck? No," Sally gritted her teeth in a whisper. Again she smiled. "Josh, my dear, do you know who the director of the rehabilitation center is?"

"I have no idea," Josh whispered back. "A friend of mine set this all up. All I knew is that he said it was for a good cause, so I said fine."

"Well then, my dear, you're in for a fairly big surprise. Shall we walk?" Sally asked as she took hold of Josh's arm, leading the way.

Once they were alone and in Josh's office, Sally sat down on the large sofa that she had once remembered as a bed. She crossed her long legs, certain Josh would comment, but he didn't.

In a rather serious tone, Josh asked, "Now that you've got my undivided attention, what don't I know?"

In a clear-cut voice, Sally resumed the conversation. "Dr. Martin Lewis happens to be the director of the Meridian Rehabilitation Center."

Josh's handsome face turned pale.

"Something wrong?" Sally asked.

Josh turned away from Sally and walked toward the window. For several moments, neither spoke.

Josh broke the silence as he walked over to Sally and stood before her like a young boy confessing. "I'm not going to ask you who told you, but I would like to explain."

"I'm listening," was Sally response.

"I know you think I'm totally full of shit, and maybe I was, but that was before Elaine. I was and still am in love with her."

Sally's mouth dropped open. "Oh my God. I certainly wasn't expecting you to say that."

Josh's face grew more serious. "Remember the day you and Elaine were here for the Fennington Show?"

Sally nodded.

"I don't think you noticed, and it appeared as if no one else did either. I couldn't take my eyes off her. Elaine was the most beautiful woman I had ever seen. I didn't know it then, but I had already fallen in love with her."

Sally was speechless. She couldn't imagine Josh Derman, one of the most eligible bachelors in Chicago, admitting his insecurities.

"I would have done anything for that woman, but she didn't even look my way. At first I thought it would be better never to see her again. I decided I could live with that decision.

"However, every night before I fell asleep, all I could think about was Elaine. As you well know, this had never happened before. Even if I was lying next to someone else, I saw Elaine's face before me.

"Then it happened. I saw Elaine again. I was at the racetrack, Arlington, with a large party of business associates. I was the host and could not leave. At that point, my heartfelt decision was meaningless. I wanted to at least say hello.

"That day did not allow me the luxury of speaking with Elaine. However, I did overhear the waiter at Elaine's table say he'd see her tomorrow.

"At first I wasn't sure that was actually what the waiter had meant to say, but the next day I arrived at the track only moments before Elaine. Strangely enough, she didn't notice me watching her.

"It was at that time when I realized she was a very unhappy woman. There was such sadness in her eyes. It wasn't only me she didn't respond to. It seemed as if from the moment she arrived, her thoughts were her own.

"I should have left well enough alone, but something about Elaine fascinated me.

"During the last race, the waiter repeated the same words to Elaine as he had said the day before. I hadn't intended on returning the next day, but I did, and so did Elaine.

"As the days passed, I had begun to fall deeper and deeper in love with Elaine. I still knew nothing about her, only that she came to the racetrack every day it was open. Although it should have, it didn't seem to matter.

"It took me a while to finally walk over to Elaine's table. When she didn't remember me, my ego was slightly wounded, but I got over all that. Especially after our first conversation."

"One thing led to another, and after several times together I had begun to feel as if Elaine was actually enjoying herself the way I had been."

Sally smiled at Josh in a somewhat comforting way. For some reason, she couldn't take her eyes off him. He actually had a tear or two running down his cheek.

From Josh's expression, Sally knew he was exposing himself in a way he had never done before.

"Sal, as you know, I've had my share of women."

Sally nodded with personal knowledge. "I don't know what to say."

"I don't either," Josh added. "I have tried to contact Elaine every day, but she will not speak to me and she refuses to let me visit. My heart is really torn. I had always intended to end our relationship before it had gotten out of hand. I've spoken with Ben Caufield, her doctor, and he tells me to be patient, so I am."

"How do you know Dr. Caufield?" Sally questioned.

"We go back awhile."

After realizing he had told Sally more than he intended, he stopped himself.

"Did you know Elaine was pregnant at the time of her suicide attempt?" Sally blurted out without thinking.

Josh was stunned by Sally's words. "No, I didn't know." Josh paced back and forth in a somewhat nervous pattern before he spoke again. "Elaine was confused and upset that day. I wish she would have let me help. I wanted to try, but she wouldn't let me into her life. There was so much I wanted to know and so much she wouldn't say. What happened to the baby?"

Sally's voice lowered. "She lost it. Elaine was a very private person who kept secrets from everyone, including Martin."

Josh nodded, recognizing an accurate statement.

"Just in case you weren't aware," Sally added, "Martin Lewis happens to be a wonderful man. There aren't many men like Martin left in this world."

"I know quite a bit about Martin Lewis," Josh said with assurance. "Elaine mentioned more than once how lucky she was to have a man like Martin loving her. Even when we made love, she mentioned Martin's kindness and how she wished she could return his love, but she couldn't."

"Spare me the details," Sally said, as she was just about ready to leave and join the others. She had heard enough.

Josh reached for the doorknob, holding onto it tightly, not letting Sally leave. "You know what's ironic?" Josh added. "I never expected any of this to happen."

Sally yanked the door open with a swing. As their eyes met for what she had thought to be the very last time, she snapped back at Josh with a chill in her voice. "No one ever does."

Chapter 16

During the next week, Elaine refused all but one appointment with Ben Caufield. At that meeting, Elaine spoke without distraction.

"I know you think that you can help me. Maybe you can, but I don't think so. I'm not sure I really want help. The past is the past and I really have no desire to go back. What's done is done. Can you understand that?"

"Yes, I can understand that," Ben responded quickly.

"Good, then we agree," Elaine said as she stood up. "I want to go back to my room. My life is my life. It's not public record or anything like that. I don't feel like reliving anything that has happened to me in the past. Got it?"

Ben leaned back against his chair, preparing to give Elaine a mini lecture. "Sometimes we have to go back before we can go forward. You, my dear, have come to the Castleberry for help. You said you would try and I believe at that time you meant it. You were not forced to come here, yet you act as if you were. What I would like is for you to go back to your room and think about helping yourself. I can't do it without you. I need your help. Do you understand?"

Elaine acknowledged Ben with a slight nod.

"Good, then we agree. That almost makes us friends," Ben added.

"I don't think so," came Elaine's blunt response.

From her words and the expression on Elaine's face, Ben could sense the complexity that hid behind those unresponsive eyes of hers.

"Now can I go back to my room?" Elaine asked again, annoyed by the delay.

"Certainly," Ben said as he buzzed for Mary Lynn.

Mary's entrance was quick. "So how did it go?" she asked Elaine, not surprised when Elaine didn't answer.

"I'm afraid Elaine has come to the conclusion that she can't be helped," Ben responded with just a hint of challenge in his voice.

"Nonsense, that's pure hogwash," Mary added. She motioned with her hand, acknowledging to Dr. Caufield that she could remedy this.

Ben nodded with a half smile, certain that Mary Lynn's dynamic vitality would be just what Elaine needed. He wondered if Mary Lynn had been aware of Elaine and the similarity between them. Maybe not, he imagined, but he certainly was.

On that same day, Ben received another call from Martin. He had tried his best to seem optimistic, but as the days passed, he hoped he wasn't leading Martin to a unrealistic conclusion.

"So how's it going?" Martin asked.

"Well, there's not much to report other than I'm trying my damnedest to get Elaine to open up. Sometimes when I look into her eyes I see the desperate part of her wanting to let go. Then there are those other times when I wonder if I can break through any of this at all."

"Maybe I can help. Please, Ben, I love her so much. I really need to see her."

"Martin, you're a great guy and you know I think the world of you, but Elaine is my patient and I have to respect her wishes. If she says no, it's no. Believe me, I would love to see how the two of you interact, but no is no. I have always tried to respect my patients' rights even if I held an opposing view."

Martin drew in a long, deep breath before speaking. "I'm sorry, Ben. I know how hard it is to get Elaine to talk about her past. Sometimes she can be very stubborn."

"You might say that," Ben agreed.

"I won't drive you crazy anymore," Martin promised. "It's just that I love her so."

"I know you do," Ben added. "Really I do."

"Will you tell her I love her?" Martin asked in a desperate tone.

"Certainly I will," Ben pledged.

Elaine didn't have lunch or dinner that day. Once again she sat by her window, talking to no one. Even when Mary came to say goodnight, she didn't respond.

Then in the morning, Elaine ate almost nothing for breakfast. The toast and tea she forced down came right back up minutes later.

After an hour or so of trying to stay awake, she dozed off. Immediately after she closed her eyes, her mind became clouded by that awful nightmare she was certain had vanished from her mind.

It was cold and very foggy. Elaine was alone at the cemetery. She looked down at the headstone, which read, "Steven Lewis, January 1, 1986 - January 1, 1986." Elaine fell to the ground. Her arms covered the tiny grave. Tears poured from her eyes as she lay down beside Stevie's grave. Her heart began beating in rapid vibrations. At that moment, she couldn't tell if she was dead or alive. Either way, it was of no consequence to her. Death might have been the relief she had hoped for.

Elaine cried out. "It's Mommy, I'm here with you. Mommy loves you. I won't let them hurt you. Nobody will make fun of you. Not my son. I love you too much."

When Mary heard Elaine's outcries, she ran to her room and pushed open the door. Mary held Elaine, trying to comfort her until she was fully awake.

With gentle movements, Mary pressed a wet cloth over Elaine's eyes. Several minutes later, a hint of color returned to Elaine's face.

Mary's words of comfort contributed to easing Elaine out of her distress. "It's alright Elaine, you're going to feel better. Everything's going to be just fine. You'll see. Just when things look the worst is when the turnabout occurs."

By this time, Elaine had claimed her senses. "My life is never going to be as it should," she cried out. "I did what I thought was best and I ruined everything."

Elaine, disgusted with herself, looked at Mary in a straightforward manner and asked, "Did you know I told everyone in our family, including Martin's mother, that my son had died during birth? How's that for motherly love?"

Mary nodded. "Yes, I was told all about that on the day you were brought in."

Elaine was surprised by all this. "You mean to say you know how horrible I am and the awful things I've done? Do you know about my sister Megan and how irresponsible a person I've been?"

Mary responded quickly, refusing to let Elaine's words pass unnoticed. "I know your complete history. So what? I'm here to help you, not judge you. We all make mistakes. That's how we learn. Don't you think I've had my share of mistakes? I was a patient here."

"You?" Elaine questioned.

"Yes, I was a mess. I never expected to recover from the trauma that surrounded me, but I've learned from my mistakes. Not exactly out of choice, but out of necessity."

Elaine shook her head. "I never learn. In fact there isn't a day that goes by that I don't stop and ask myself why I am so selfish. I never think of anyone other than myself."

Elaine became restless as she lay on the bed, tossing, mumbling and turning back and forth. "I don't understand why you don't hate me. You should, everyone should. I'm a horrible person who ruins lives."

"You know something Elaine, I've never been in favor of people feeling sorry for themselves. I've yet to see that solve a problem. As far as I can see, the only one who hates you is you, and that has to stop."

Elaine was slightly taken back by Mary's bluntness. She didn't know how to respond to such direct truth.

"When will the pain go away?" Elaine asked. "I want the pain to leave. I can't stand it one more day."

With all her knowledge and sincerity, Mary took hold of Elaine's hand and squeezed tightly. "Pain doesn't just go away like a bad cold. Sometimes it can last forever. You have the power to let it go, but ultimately, it's your decision. You've got to stop looking back and prepare to look ahead. Stop feeling sorry for yourself."

"Is that what you think this is?" Elaine's voice lashed back.

"You tell me," Mary insisted.

Before responding to Mary's last question, Elaine thought for a moment. "I'm not feeling sorry for myself. I'm feeling sorry for everyone who cares about me. I don't deserve anyone's love."

"You most definitely do. The only thing wrong with this picture is you. Stop being so dammed hard on yourself. You can make the difference. You can unchain yourself. It's been a long time. Don't you think it's time to come back into the world?" Mary asked with concern.

By this time, Elaine had become very tired. She knew that she would disappoint Mary with her answer. So, for the time being, she decided not to answer at all.

Before Mary left, she grasped Elaine's hands and stood directly in front of her, speaking with grave concern. "Give yourself a chance."

"What if I don't want to?" Elaine argued.

"Do it anyway," Mary said, smiling with a gentle frankness.

***

"Do you still think I'm a bitch?" Elaine asked as she took a seat on Ben's couch.

"Do you think you're a bitch?" Ben responded to her candid question.

Elaine bit down on her lip and thought before answering. "As a matter of fact, I think I'm a whole lot worse than that."

"Well you're not," Ben said with obvious, incontestable certainty.

"Do you really think so?" Elaine asked.

"Yes, I do. But it's you who ultimately has to believe that."

"I wish it were all that easy," Elaine said as she stood up, walked across the room and leaned on his desk. "In the morning, I wake up hating myself and in the evening, before I go to bed, I pray that when morning comes everything will change. But it never does."

Ben sat back in his chair, watching Elaine pace back and forth, apparently having more to say. He was puzzled by her sudden outburst upon entering his office. Routinely getting her to say anything had been like pulling teeth.

Their conversation was interrupted by a phone call. Ben Caufield excused himself as he went to a private office next door.

While he was gone, Elaine sat back down on the couch, crossing her right leg over her left and then reversing. She nervously stood up and then down as she waited.

The voice in the other end was familiar. "Ben, it's Josh Derman. I hope I wasn't interrupting anything too important. This just couldn't wait."

"So, what can I do for you?" Ben asked.

"Can I come out to see Elaine? I really need to see her."

"Josh, I'm afraid it just wouldn't be feasible. She's not ready. You know I can't betray a patient's privacy."

"That's okay, Ben. I understand. I was hoping Elaine's situation would change. Again, I'm sorry for bothering you."

Josh hung up, embarrassed for calling. He should have known better.

When Ben returned to his office, Elaine had left a note on his desk. Ben read the letter.

I'm sorry for my outburst today. I'm going back to my room to try and figure out just why I did it. — Elaine

Chapter 17

Sally had been sipping her morning coffee slower than usual. She was trying her damnedest to get used to being a woman alone. It had been well over a year since her divorce became final but, in the loneliness of her own company, she still had regrets. Not having children was her main grievance.

Sally was grateful when the telephone rang.

"How about dinner tonight?" the voice on the other end asked.

At first Sally didn't recognize the voice. When she didn't respond, the caller asked another question.

"Is that a yes or a no?" he asked.

Sally smiled when she recognized Josh's voice. "Josh, it's you."

"It sure the hell is," Josh responded in his usual jaunty spirit.

"'Hello, how are you' might have been a better way to start, don't you think?" Sally asked.

"It's Friday. I never think on Friday," Josh said with a splash of his usual vitality.

"Well, in that case, I always say yes on Friday. What time?" Sally asked.

Josh ended the conversation with an easy, "How does eight sound?"

Sally, wanting to say never mind, responded, "Sounds good to me. See you then."

After hanging up the phone, Sally continued sipping her coffee, but this time she didn't feel so lonely.

***

Josh didn't arrive until ten. He looked extremely appealing in his jeans and white shirt. Sally should have slammed the door in his face, but she didn't. She couldn't.

Because he brought flowers, candy and his adorable smile with him, she let him in.

They never did have dinner. Not because he was late, but because they both knew what they wanted of each other. Even when they were seeing each other on a regular basis they never made love, but they did have great sex.

That night it wasn't fun like it used to be, or even the slightest bit sensuous. Josh wasn't the same lover he used to be. He had changed. Love can do that to you, she thought. For a moment or two, she was jealous of Elaine, but that passed when reality brought her back to Elaine's desperate situation.

Sally decided next time Josh called, she would say no. At the same time, Josh made a decision. He wouldn't call again.

Chapter 18

It didn't take long for Elaine to consider Mary's words meaningful. Several days later, during one of Elaine's therapy sessions, she decided to confront the issue of what had gotten into her the other day.

"You know, Doctor, sometimes I just feel like letting off steam. Is that going to be alright with you?"

"It most certainly is," Ben said, delighted she wanted to. "Anytime you feel like letting off steam, you go right ahead and do it. That's what I'm here for."

Ben watched Elaine as she took a deep breath, convinced that she was about to let off some steam. But she didn't.

Instead, Elaine got up off the couch and walked toward the door. "Thanks," she said. "It's nice to know that I don't have any restrictions. You might not understand it, but that really makes me feel better."

Just when Ben had a reason to believe a breakthrough had begun to unfold, Elaine refused to eat, shower or attend her therapy sessions. They were once again back at square one.

Several days had passed. Martin and Josh called every day, but Ben did not tell them what had happened. He had decided to wait it out, hoping this was just a minor setback. Elaine had them before.

Every morning, Mary got Elaine out of bed, showered her and then helped her dress. She brought a breakfast tray into her room and was not satisfied until Elaine had taken at least three bites of toast and several sips of orange juice. Some days it was almost noon before the three bites of toast were eaten and the sips of orange juice swallowed, but Mary was persistent.

This routine lasted for nearly a week. It was early Sunday morning that Elaine sat on her bed waiting for Mary. When Mary entered the room, she was momentarily speechless. Elaine had showered and dressed herself.

"This is the first Sunday in years that I have not gone to Mass. There is a God," Mary cried in relief as she ran over to Elaine and gave her the tightest hug she could.

Elaine held onto Mary's hug for a long time. Once the tears stopped, she let go.

***

"Did you know that I fell in love with a man I barely knew? Mac, yes, Mac Porter was his name." Those were the first words out of Elaine's mouth during her next therapy session.

As always, Ben answered with a similar question. "Was I supposed to?"

Elaine gave an impatient shrug. "Guess not."

"Does that bother you?" Ben asked.

"No, not really. I don't even know why I asked such a ridiculous question. Or, for that matter, why I even mentioned Mac's name."

"I assume because either you really thought I knew or you really wanted to talk about it. Am I right?" Ben asked.

Elaine became slightly perturbed. "Now why in hell would that bother me? And why would I want to talk about Mac? It was just something that happened, no big deal. What's love anyway? Easy come, easier go."

Ben immediately got hold of the situation, realizing what he had there was potentially dangerous. "Mac? Who is Mac?"

Elaine had promised herself never to discuss Mac with anyone. Why now, she thought. By this time, her head was swimming with thoughts and ideas.

Ben recognized Elaine's confusion, so before things got out of hand, he offered her a way out. "Maybe it would be better if we discussed this later. After all, we have time. No need to rush. What do you say we stop for today? There's always tomorrow."

Elaine's pattern of speech became frantic. "Maybe not. Maybe this is all there is and there won't be a tomorrow. If I don't talk about Mac soon, I think I'm going to explode. I think it should be now, right now."

Ben leaned back against his chair, waiting for Elaine to state her mind. He wouldn't let her go too far.

All of a sudden, strange and bizarre as it was, Elaine began her journey. Or at least what Ben had imagined it to be.

"I really don't know how this whole thing started. Well, maybe I do," Elaine said, ready to begin.

Unexpectedly, Elaine clammed up. She became agitated and unsure, not unusual for her. "What if I change my mind and don't really want to talk about this right now?"

Ben's response was quick. "Then you won't. The conversation will end whenever you decide."

Elaine nodded her head slightly. Without warning, she walked out the door.

After she left, Ben sat for a while, wondering why he just couldn't get Elaine to feel free enough to let go. He was failing and he didn't like it.

Whenever they were close to a breakthrough, Elaine would either clam up or storm out of his office.

Later, Elaine walked back in unannounced. Ben didn't appear shocked.

"If you haven't guessed, I like to control the conversation, or at least that's the way I was when I was younger," Elaine said as she sat herself down on the couch.

She continued her rebellious outburst. "That was when life seemed to have so much to offer. I used to think once I grew up there would be chances out there for me to take. But then it happened. Bad luck had found me. It just never seemed to stop coming."

Ben didn't respond, he just listened as Elaine continued.

"Did you know it was my fault about Stevie? I was his mother. I gave birth to him. I lied to everyone, but I couldn't lie to myself. God knows I tried. I'm pathetic. I failed and then I pulled away. I'm unfit. That's what they'll say if they find out."

"Why don't you tell me who exactly they are?" was Ben's immediate response.

"Everyone," she added. "Everyone."

"Why does that bother you so?"

Elaine lashed back in anger. "Wouldn't it bother you?"

"Maybe it would, but certainly there had to be something good in your life to give you balance."

"Balance? What balance could there be? I had done a terrible thing, so why should any good come to me?"

"Why don't you answer that?" Ben asked.

"No, I don't think I will," Elaine said as she rested her head back against the sofa.

Silence lengthened between them.

Elaine stood up and walked to the door. Before she left, a faint smile appeared on Elaine's rather drawn-out face. "And then I met Mac. The timing was perfect. We needed each other."

For a moment or two, Elaine didn't speak. Ben watched her as she silently fought with herself, walking back into the room.

Another outburst surprised Ben.

"Before that, I met Josh. He wasn't perfect but he was funny. I hadn't laughed in such a very long time. I guess I shouldn't have involved him, but I did. I wasn't thinking. So, again I had done something so wrong. Josh had become attached while I became even more lonely. How could any of this have happened? I had a wonderful husband who loved me, certainly more than I deserved. It didn't matter if Martin ever found out. I had to live with the horrors that lie in my heart. I just couldn't."

Elaine walked over toward Ben's desk. She pressed her fingertips on his desk and leaned toward him, looking at him eye-to-eye. "What the hell is wrong with me?"

Ben could sense Elaine was much more distressed than he had imagined. "Well, now that you've opened up a bit, maybe I can help you with your pain," he said, figuring it was worth a try.

Elaine's eyes held caution. "I'm afraid we've only touched the surface. You know what would have made everything seem so much better?"

Ben drew in a deep breath before speaking. "No, I don't."

"Well, I do," Elaine said right before she walked out the door. "Death."

Quickly, Ben dialed his phone. "Please tell Mary Lynn I need to see her."

"How did it go?" Mary asked as she sat herself down on the small stool beside Ben's desk.

"Not too good. We took two steps forward and four steps back. Every time I think I'm going to be able to help her, she swings to the other side and I can't seem to do a thing."

"Don't worry Ben," Mary sighed. "We're going to do it. You'll see. This is where faith comes in."

"I certainly hope you're right," Ben added.

Mary spoke within herself. "Me too."

***

Later that evening, Elaine sat in the lounge, pretending to watch TV. Her mind was as far away as one could get in a seated position. Her thoughts distanced her from her surroundings and, as usual, she kept to herself.

Several other patients were off to the side playing Scrabble, a common way to pass the time.

A young woman approached Elaine. She was very petite, almost flowerlike, and her eyes were saddened by time.

The woman, unsure of Elaine, sat down beside her. "Would you like some company?" she asked.

Elaine, who either didn't hear the woman or chose not to, didn't answer.

The woman repeated, "Would you like some company, or do you always like to be alone?"

Elaine didn't like the interruption, but she answered. "I really don't know. I never really thought about it."

"Well, it certainly seems like that to me," was the young woman's honest observation.

Elaine's eyes deepened as she spoke. "How in the world would you know anything about me?"

"I know what I see. You don't talk to any of us. In fact, we weren't even sure you could talk."

Elaine was slightly annoyed. "I didn't know anyone was watching me. And just who are we?"

"Well, if you haven't discovered it yet, there's not a whole hell of a lot to do here. All we have is each other," she said, pointing to the others. "I don't know if we're friends or not, but whatever we are to each other, we're all we've got. Can we count you in?" the young woman asked.

"I don't think so," Elaine said as she hunched back against the couch. "I'm not very good company these days."

The young woman graciously stood up. "I understand how you feel, but if you change your mind I'll be around. Doesn't look like I'll be touring Europe or anything like that. By the way, let me introduce myself," she said as she extended her hand for a handshake. "I'm Jessie Rogers."

Elaine nodded as she shook her hand. "I'm Elaine Lewis."

"I know," Jessie said as she returned to her Scrabble game.

***

After that evening, Elaine chose not to go into the lounge. Friendships, even short-term ones, seemed too taxing for Elaine.

On Friday morning, Jessie stood outside of Elaine's room, wondering if she should knock. She was just about ready to walk away when Mary approached her from behind.

"Morning hon," Mary cheerfully said as she proceeded to walk down the hall.

Jessie called out to her. "Do you think Elaine will have breakfast with the rest of us?"

Mary turned around to answer her. "I don't think so, but it's worth a try. Wouldn't it be great if she did?"

Jessie knocked on the door with soft, unassuming taps. When Elaine didn't answer, Jessie opened the door and walked in.

"Mary, is that you?" a voice called out from the shower.

Jessie didn't answer. Instead, she sat by the window in Elaine's chair.

Elaine was startled by Jessie's presence. "What are you doing here?" she asked, slightly annoyed.

"I've come to invite you to breakfast."

Elaine shook her head. "I don't think so. Not today. It's not like it's a party or anything like that."

Jessie had decided not to accept no for an answer. There was a dead, heated stare between the two of them. Jessie spoke first. "I'm not going to take no for an answer. Besides, what else have you got to do?"

"I have nothing to do, but I really don't see that it's any of your concern," Elaine said as she stood by the door, motioning with her hands for Jessie to leave.

"Don't you ever get sick of eating alone?" Jessie asked with curious eyes.

"No, not really," Elaine responded. "As I told you the other evening, I am not very good company. I don't like to talk about myself."

Jessie gave Elaine a brief but understanding smile. "Neither do I. We can talk about the weather, the news or whatever."

Elaine shook her head. "No, really, I prefer to have breakfast in my room."

"Okay, then what do you say I have my breakfast in here with you?" Jessie said, leaving no room for a no.

Elaine shrugged her shoulders. "I guess it would alright. But if you're expecting light-hearted chitchat, you've come to the wrong place."

Jessie seemed content with Elaine's approval. "Sounds good to me," she said. "You said wrong place, but I say it's the right place."

As it happened, Jessie was right. After that first, uncomfortable breakfast, Elaine and Jessie were inseparable. They had seemed to find in each other what the other one lacked. They seemed to connect and respond to each other as friends.

At first their conversations were insignificant, but as the days passed and comfort set in, on occasion one or the other unchained a story out of sequence.

One morning at breakfast, Jessie knocked on Elaine's door, only to be surprised by her not being there. Lying on Elaine's bed was a note.

Dear Jess,

I decided to take you up on your invitation to break-fast. I'm in the main dining room. Better late than never.

Before going into the dining room, Jessie stopped at the nurse's station. She looked around for Mary, but she was nowhere to be found. Just as she was about to leave, Mary came up to her with a smile from ear to ear. "Well, you did it. Our friend is in the dining room."

Jessie was pleased. "Can you believe it?" she asked Mary.

Mary smiled in relief. "I don't know how you did it, but am I glad you did. Go join your friend. I think she's waiting for you."

Jessie was delighted when she saw Elaine seated at her table. She quickly ran over to Elaine. "Well, you made it. So how does it feel to be among the living?"

A brief smile appeared on Elaine's face. "Actually, it's not as bad as I thought. Really it isn't."

Jessie smiled and reached for a muffin. "Shall I introduce you to the others?"

"Later would be better," Elaine explained. "So how was your night?"

Jessie's lips parted as she spoke. "Another rough one. It's those damn dreams. I wish to God they'd go away. But they never do. What about you? Any dreams?"

Elaine's face lit up. "No, not lately. As a matter of fact, I slept great. Being with you and being able to talk so freely certainly has helped. I've never had anyone to talk to who could feel my pain the way you do."

"You're right about that," Jessie agreed. "We're like an old pair of shoes. Sometimes the shoemaker can fix the shoes, sometimes he can't. But if not, the shoes get tossed away. Do you think we'll be like those shoes, tossed aside and forgotten?"

Elaine shrugged her shoulders as she looked at her friend in a very serious way. "I don't know. Really I don't, but I'd like to think the shoemaker might help us get a comfortable fit."

"Me too," Jessie added.

Chapter 19

It was almost seven in the morning when Maggie became concerned as to why Martin had not come down for his coffee. Generally, by that time he had already had his two cups of coffee and the paper had been read from first page to last.

Maggie stood outside Martin's bedroom door for several minutes before knocking. When she finally did decide to knock, she was relieved to hear Martin's voice. "Come in," he said.

Maggie silently hoped her shock at Martin's appearance wouldn't transpose to her face. "Good morning," she said as she placed the mug of hot coffee on his night table.

Martin's eyes were a bit more red than usual, but what was most unexpected was he hadn't even been out of bed. That was reason enough to worry.

There he sat and, for the first time, the stress he faced began to surface.

"Have a seat," Martin said as he took a sip of coffee.

"Are you alright?" Maggie asked. Judging from his appearance, she knew he wasn't.

"Yes, I'm fine. I just needed a little extra sleep. I had a restless night but nevertheless, my eyes did finally close around four."

"Well, that's good. I was beginning to worry, but if you say you're fine, then you are," Maggie added, hoping that would trigger a more truthful response.

"Well, maybe I'm not so fine," Martin conceded. "Maybe I'm even horrible. I really don't know exactly what the hell I am, but what I do know is I'm lonely, very lonely."

"Give yourself some time," Maggie said as she sat down on the chair beside his bed. "Sometimes time is the greatest healer of all."

"I don't know. I thought I could handle this. I thought I could handle anything," Martin's voice peaked. "But I don't know. I'm tired of pretending my life is okay. My life is shit and there doesn't seem to be a thing I can do to change it. Why is it that love changes?"

Maggie didn't respond for a moment or two, but then she knew it was time say her piece. "Martin, you know I love you. You're the son I never had. I have seen you go through probably more tragedy than most. But what has always kept me in awe of you has been your kindness to others."

Martin didn't interrupt. He just listened as Maggie continued.

"Despite what you think, there does come a time when you have to pay a little more attention to your own needs. I think now is the time for Martin Lewis to start caring about himself."

"What are you suggesting?" Martin asked with interest.

"That you stop being so hard on yourself. Let go, just a bit. It's okay to get mad and express what you feel. Stop holding your feelings inside. Let yourself get mad."

"I am mad," Martin shouted.

Maggie seemed pleased as his voice got louder. "Good," she said. "Let it go."

"I tried to understand why Elaine couldn't accept Stevie, but I couldn't. The worst part of it all was lying to my mother. How could I have deprived my mother of her grandson? What was I thinking? I should be the one at the Castleberry Pavilion. What kind of a man does this make me?"

Maggie had to interrupt. "It makes you the best kind of man. You responded to your wife's needs. You did what you thought to be the best decision at the time."

"But was it?" Martin questioned her.

"I don't know," Maggie added with sincerity. "Sometimes we respond to a situation without thinking about the consequences. That's what makes us human."

"I only prolonged the inevitable," Martin admitted.

Maggie's voice angered. "You did what you thought was right. This wasn't your fault."

"How can you be so sure of this?" Martin asked.

"Because you're not God. The ultimate decisions are made by him, so stop blaming yourself."

"I can't seem to do that."

Once again, Maggie raised her voice. "But you've got to."

"I'm so dammed scared I'll lose again. After Iris and Becky were killed, I promised myself never to love again. I should have left well enough alone."

Maggie's tone softened. "Loving is good. A life without love would truly be lonely. That wouldn't be right for a man like you."

"I need some questions answered," Martin cried out.

Maggie reached for Martin's hand and squeezed it tightly. "Some questions don't have answers. So please, stop doing this to yourself. You have to be there for your wife. She's going to need you."

"That's if she comes home. She might choose not to."

"You're a good man and, believe me, no woman wants to lose a man like you."

Maggie was standing by the door, ready to leave, when Martin called to her. "Do you realize how special you are?"

Maggie smiled. "I'm flattered, but I'm really not very special at all," she said. "I'm just here for you as I always will be. Right now, I think you should get dressed and make your hospital rounds. Your patients need you."

Martin couldn't help but add one last thought. "I think you're one of God's angels and don't try to tell me any different."

Chapter 20

Jessie's friendship seemed to be the inspiration Elaine had needed to begin her healing. Ben Caufield had been just as astonished as Martin was when he heard the good news.

Not only had Elaine's private sessions with Ben become extremely productive, but the mere fact that Elaine had agreed to group sessions was quite a turning point. Still, it was the private sessions that became most insightful.

"Why the racetrack?" Ben asked Elaine, trusting the timing was right.

Judging by Elaine's facial expression and the unspoken pain and anger in her eyes, he wasn't exactly certain she would answer. At first, Ben thought he had pushed too hard. Sometimes he did that, especially when he felt a breakthrough could be a possibility.

Elaine sat across from Ben with a blank stare for quite some time before answering. Then it was as if a volcano burst from within her.

"As soon as I neared the track, suddenly I was relieved. Nobody knew me, but more important than that, nobody cared. I was just a face without a name. I wasn't a wife or mother. I was just there. The track was the only place I could rest my mind. I didn't think about Martin, Stevie or Megan. The only thing that mattered was the racing, and after a time, that didn't even matter."

Ben sat back as he watched Elaine's every move. He didn't speak, certain the mood would be broken if he did. He just listened and learned as much about Elaine as she would allow him to. Until that day, she rarely allowed herself to be exposed.

Elaine kept right on talking and Ben kept right on listening. Ben realized his previous question gave her an opportune time to respond, which he seemed content with.

"Sometimes I wasn't even sure I liked the track. That was near the beginning, when I would skip a day or two. But after being there, the dislike passed. I liked having a place to go where nothing mattered. I didn't care if I won or lost. It wasn't about winning."

Elaine sat down for a moment. Ben wasn't sure if she had finished or not, so he remained silent, waiting for Elaine's next move. There wasn't one. She left his office without saying good-bye. That was typical.

***

During their next session, Ben once again took a chance. It was the days when Elaine would show up for her session and not communicate that made Ben go one step beyond.

"What do you remember most about your father?" Ben asked with interest. Once before, he had tried to recall these feelings in Elaine, but he failed. However, he never gave up the effort.

"I remember the way he smelled. It was god-awful. Sometimes the smell of alcohol lingered in our house even when he was away."

So far so good, Ben thought, deciding to go further. "Any pleasant memories of your father?"

Elaine responded quickly. "No, not a one."

"Before you say no, think about it," Ben responded aggressively.

Elaine's eyes widened. "I couldn't stand the man. So why in hell would there be anything pleasant about him or anything he had done that I would want to remember?"

Ben nodded. Realizing he was about to lose the hand he was playing, he stopped in a dead, fast manner.

A moment or two later, Elaine waved goodbye. Next thing Ben knew, she was gone. Not exactly a surprise, he thought.

Elaine didn't return to her room just yet. She stood outside of Ben's office, trying to remember something good about her father. She nervously paced back and forth, trying to remember something, even if it was insignificant. At first she drew a blank, but then it came to her. The bracelet. Yes, she thought, the bracelet was good.

She knocked on Ben's door. He responded immediately. "Come in."

She did. He was glad.

"There was one memory," Elaine's voice was loud. "It was the night of my grammar school graduation. I had always admired my grandmother's pearl bracelet. She had promised it to me the day before she died. My father told me that he would give it to me when he thought it was the right time. Time had passed and I was certain that he had forgotten. That night he handed me a small, black box. My heart pounded with excitement as I looked inside. There it was, exactly the way I remembered it. I put it on and wore it proudly. In fact, I wore it the entire month and then some."

***

Session after session, Elaine continued to let go of memories that had always come between her and happiness. She had begun to trust Ben, but not enough to be completely honest.

Ben was certain that between the lost details and the subject matter Elaine chose to discuss, something would lead him to the light in the tunnel.

Elaine maintained a level of trust with her peers during group therapy, but she still hadn't come to the point where she was willing to completely let go.

Personally, Ben was trying his damnedest to weave Elaine's mother into their conversation. When he tried, Elaine resisted. She would either leave or completely clam up.

Then one day, toward the end of a private session, Elaine shouted out loudly, "Sometimes I would like to be a child again."

Ben took a deep breath. This breakthrough had been long overdue. "Exactly why is that?"

"Because," she cried out, "I never got the chance to do the things young girls do. I even had to take Megan to the library while I studied. I never had time for friends, dances, movies or sleepovers. Don't get me wrong, it wasn't that I didn't love my sister. I did. But sometimes, I just wanted to be like the other kids."

"And you couldn't?" Ben asked with sincerity.

"Never," Elaine replied. "Megan was my responsibility. Wherever I went Megan went, except for school."

"And you resented Megan because of it?" Ben added with caution.

"Absolutely not. Megan was such a sweet girl. She couldn't help what her situation was. She was brought into the world that way. So why hate her? No, it was my mother I hated." Elaine placed her hand over her mouth in embarrassment. "I shouldn't have said that, should I?"

By this time, Elaine had started to cry. Ben didn't stop her, not this time. Stopping her now would ruin the momentum.

"Anyway, if my mother wouldn't have expected me to do all the mothering, maybe, yes maybe, Megan would be alive today," Elaine cried out.

Ben was slightly apprehensive to stop for even a moment, afraid the conversation might end.

Elaine continued while Ben listened to her every word, hoping that all the hatred Elaine had bottled up inside her would surface. The evidence was there. Elaine was arguing with herself.

The words didn't stop. "You know something, Doctor? Sometimes when I think back, I don't really remember having a mother. In fact, I think I was a mother to Megan in every sense of the word. Most days I fed her breakfast, lunch and dinner. I bathed her, loved her and I damned well took care of her. I did everything a mother was supposed to do. And on the days when I didn't feel like caring for Megan, I had no choice. I just did it anyway. None of this was her fault."

This session of therapy was going very well. However, Ben still proceeded with caution. "Did you ever try to talk to your mother?"

Elaine answered with a rather ugly grin. "Lenore Foster didn't have to answer to me or, for that matter, anyone else. Every day was the same. No changes were ever made."

Ben was just about ready to ask another question when Elaine stood up and shouted. "I guess you think I didn't love my mother. How could you, especially since I just said I hated her?"

"Did you?" Ben asked.

"Did I hate her or love her, you ask? I don't really know. I never gave it too much thought. By the time my chores were done and Megan was asleep, I was too tired to care about anything, let alone my feelings."

"Where was your father during all of this?" Ben inquired.

"My father was drunk. I never really knew if my father was drunk because of my mother's inconsiderate behavior or her behavior was because my father drank. Whatever the reason, I hated my life. I was going to have the perfect life. Children, lots of them, and a husband who loved me. But when the fairytale began, I never expected Stevie to be part of it. My dreams were shattered. What if he would die in my care? Then what? Look at my sister. I let her down. I let her die."

Ben leaned back in his chair to think for a moment. Timing was everything. He decided to ask the one question that could and might send Elaine flying out of his office like a bat out of hell.

"So that's why you're afraid to let yourself love anyone, isn't it? After all, it's hard to give of yourself, don't you think? Maybe even selfish, wouldn't you say?"

Elaine didn't explode or run out of the room. Instead, she sat down on the chair beside Ben and looked at him straight on. By this time, tears were streaming down her face. "Oh my God, yes. Yes."

Elaine sat there for several minutes, shivering and very fatigued. Shadows deepened under her eyes as she stood up to leave the room.

Ben also stood. "Elaine," he called to her as she was leaving. "Please wait." After a session like that, Ben usually had to say a word or two. Sessions like that weren't easy and he knew it. "Are you okay?" he asked with shocking concern.

Elaine nodded in acknowledgement. "Yes, I am."

"Good," Ben said as he added one last thought. "I think today might very well be a day you will long remember."

Elaine stood on her toes, reached up toward Ben's cheek and gave him a kiss. What really surprised Ben was the smile she gave him as she left his office. "I think you might be right," she said as she walked away.

Ben stood outside his office, watching Elaine walk down the hall with a great sense of achievement.

As it happened, Mary had heard Elaine's parting words. "You must feel pretty good today," she said to Ben in passing.

With a grin on his face and quite a good feeling in his heart, he added, "You bet, Mary Lynn, you bet."

That evening, Ben had stopped by Elaine's room to check in on her. He had always made it his business to follow through on conclusive sessions where progress was made.

Sometimes after a grueling day, a patient would want to make contact with their doctor, but they won't necessarily ask to see him. Usually they don't have the strength. Ben was very aware of that enigma. Actually, it was just that which made him quite special.

Elaine sat on the edge of her bed, holding her pillow in a tight crunch. When she noticed Ben standing at her door, she felt relieved. He sensed that.

"Hello, Doctor. I'm really glad to see you. I wanted to tell you if Martin should ask about me, tell him I'm feeling better. That is, if he should ask."

Ben couldn't help but smile. "If he should ask, you say?"

"Yes, you know what I mean. He must be wondering how I am. At least I thought so."

"You might say that," Ben responded. "Martin calls here every day, sometimes twice."

Elaine seemed shocked. "He does?"

"He most certainly does. You have a husband who loves you very much."

"He's a good man, isn't he?" Elaine said with confidence, certainly not expecting an answer.

"Did you want to see him?"

Elaine hesitated for a moment before answering. "No, I don't think so. Not yet."

"Just say the word and I'll tell him," Ben added before leaving.

"Doctor?" Elaine called out.

"What can I do for you?" Ben asked.

Elaine wasn't exactly sure how to ask the next question, but somehow she managed to get the words out. "Has anyone else been asking about me?"

"Are you sure you want to know?"

"Yes, I think so," she said with a bit of reservation in her voice.

"Josh Derman called."

"Once?" she asked.

"No," Ben answered. "Every day."

Elaine was even more shocked by Josh's calls than Martin's. "Oh, I see. I really feel bad about leaving Josh to pick up the pieces. I really don't remember too much of that night. But, I guess he doesn't hate me if he called."

Ben stepped back into her room. He decided to continue the theme one step further. "I'm going to tell you something because I think you should know."

"Is it bad?" Elaine asked, unaware of exactly the impact Ben's next few words would have on her.

"Mac Porter called the other day," he added in a slow, easy voice.

Elaine's eyes filled with tears. "Mac called? I can't imagine how he found out where I was. He spoiled the promise we made to each other."

"If it will make you feel any better, he said almost the same sentiments," Ben added.

Elaine took in a deep breath. "I don't know what to say."

Ben walked back to her and, in a very sensitive way, gathered his thoughts. "Right now I don't think you should have to say anything. Try to get some rest. You've had quite a day. We'll continue tomorrow."

Elaine nodded in agreement. She then fell back against her pillow. She didn't want to dream of Mac that night, but she did.

Chapter 21

After several phone calls from Mac soliciting his plans to see Elaine, Ben flatly refused. Despite Ben's decision, Mac refused to take no for an answer, which explained his unexpected visit to the Castleberry.

It was early Saturday morning when Mac walked into Ben's office for the very first time. As early as his first hello, Mac knew he would somehow see Elaine. That was why he came and, if he didn't get to see her because of protocol, he would stay until he did.

Ben wasn't at all surprised by Mac's visit. They engaged in what most would deem a heated conversation. Being the hard-nosed therapist he was, Ben won the debate. Mac agreed to return only at Elaine's request. But it was too late. As Ben and Mac were conversing outside, Elaine happened to come across them, only moments before Mac had agreed to leave.

Mac held out his arms as Elaine fell into them. It was just as perfect as one might imagine. It was as if Elaine had always belonged in Mac's arms. Once he realized he had lost the battle, Ben returned to his office.

Mary, who had been watching from the office window, waited for Ben. "So, now what?" Mary asked the minute Ben walked in.

"I was at the front desk when he came in. He looked so determined, like a man on a mission."

"Oh, but he was. In fact, I was very surprised when he agreed to wait until Elaine was ready. I think he really is in love with Elaine," Ben said with confidence. He shook his head, puzzled by the situation. "Three men, all in love with the same woman. Each offering her what she can't give herself."

"And that is?" Mary asked, slightly bewildered by all of this.

"Happiness. Elaine wants to disregard all the tools that could make her unhappy. She looks for distractions, hoping that she can forget all the memories that make her feel sad. She's holding onto all those bad memories, leaving virtually no room for a new start."

Mary didn't respond. Her thoughts remained quietly tucked away in her heart.

"Sometimes she drinks, other times she gambles, and then there are the more serious times when she reaches out for love so completely she forgets everything else. And, my dear Mary Lynn, you and I both know her past will always be part of her future," Ben concluded.

"What can we do?" Mary asked, more concerned than ever.

"We wait."

"This may very well be a blessing," Mary said as she clenched her cross to her chest, praying silently.

"I really don't know if Elaine is ready for this confrontation or, for that matter, any other," a concerned Ben added. "But when I saw the look in Mac's eyes and the urgency in the way Elaine ran to him, I couldn't very well keep them apart."

***

At first, Elaine felt a little awkward, but then it all seemed so right. "How did you find me?" she asked with inquisitive concern.

"It wasn't easy, but after a tour like I had in 'Nam, nothing seems to be out of reach. It doesn't matter how I found you, it only matters that I did."

"What about our promise?" Elaine had to ask.

"I had to see you. I tried to forget you, but I couldn't. I wanted to thank you for letting me love you."

They walked around the Pavilion for a very long time, this time acquainting themselves to each of their pasts. What had once been an uncomplicated acquaintance suddenly began to be so much more. It was never going to be remembered as a one-night stand or, for that matter, ever forgotten.

Elaine eased into holding Mac's arm as they walked on, each quietly contemplating what would happen next. For several minutes, neither spoke.

Finally, Elaine broke the ice. "I want to kiss you and tell you everything that I've never told anyone before. I want to love you as I've never loved anyone before, but I can't. It just isn't possible."

Mac immediately stopped walking. "I know that. I came here today to make you love me the way I love you. I want you to feel the passion I feel, but now that I'm here, I know that will never be possible. I think we both know that."

Mac kissed Elaine. His large hand held her chin in a soft but gentle way. "Please forgive me for once again intruding in your life. Now that I'm here, I feel so selfish. But most of all, I feel very foolish. Maybe another time or some other place, but not now. Someday I know we will be together again."

At that moment, after listening to Mac's words, Elaine wanted to grab Mac's arm and walk away from the Castleberry and everything else she knew. That was an impossibility, but the desire was there.

She watched as Mac walked away, wondering if she would ever see him again.

***

After that day, Elaine didn't want to discuss Mac with Ben or anyone else. Along with her silence came her renewed refusal to attend group therapy.

She didn't forfeit her therapy sessions with Ben, but the openness they shared had somehow gone by the wayside. Elaine had regressed and, once again, Ben and Elaine were back to the beginning. Sometimes she talked, but for the most part, their sessions had not been very productive.

Elaine went along with all the motions. She ate breakfast, lunch and dinner. She bathed and dressed herself, but very rarely did Elaine smile.

Jessica and Elaine spent several hours a day together. Ben would watch them talk, but he imagined Jessica did most of the talking while Elaine listened. He chose not to violate their privacy. He seemed satisfied that Elaine could find refuge talking with Jessica.

There had been other variations. Josh had finally stopped calling, but Martin grew more impatient as the days passed. Ben wondered how much longer it would be until Martin did exactly as Mac had done. Their personalities were quite different, but the intensity of their love for Elaine was the same.

Ben had expected Mac to get in touch with him, but he hadn't. He wondered if the impression he had of Mac had been wrong. Sometimes his intuition wasn't as acute as he imagined it to be.

During that next month, Elaine had several bad days. Ben had become concerned, but he tried his best to hide his feelings when he spoke to Martin. Once again, waiting was their game.

***

Late one early June afternoon, Elaine sat in her favorite chair, looking out the window. She responded to a knock on her door. "Come in," she called out in a quiet whisper.

Jessie stuck her head in the doorway. "Are you sure?"

"Of course. Have a seat," Elaine said as she motioned for Jessie to sit on the edge of her bed.

Jessie flopped down on the bed and crossed her legs before speaking. "I feel like it's time to start telling you the truth."

Elaine seemed surprised. "Haven't you been?"

"Partially, but you see, I've never had a friend like you. For the first time in my life, I feel safe. I feel as if I can tell you the truth."

Elaine nodded, completely cognizant of what Jessie had said.

Jessie paused for a moment to take a breath. "Well, here goes nothing."

Suddenly, instead of talking in her usual, simple but direct style, Jessie blurted out her words in an agitated, rather loud voice.

"My son's name was David. He's not alive like I said he was. I was in the house when the fire started. At first I didn't see the smoke, but then it was all too horrible. Smoke was everywhere. I ran to David's room and grabbed him out of his crib. I couldn't see a thing. I ran for the stairs and that's when..."

Again, Jessie paused. Elaine didn't respond in any way. She waited for Jessie to continue.

Finally she did. "I remember the smoke making it very difficult for me to see, but that didn't stop me. Nothing could. All I could think about was getting David out of there. David was nestled in my arms. That's when they say I fell. By the time help came, it was too late. He was gone."

Before Jessie could get another word out, Elaine gasped, "What are you saying?"

Jessie's voice angered. "David was dead. Oh my God. Why didn't I die? I should have died. He was only a baby. My David..."

Elaine was speechless and unsure of herself. There just didn't seem to be any words that could possibly ease her friend's pain.

Jessie's voice was filled with anguish. "So you see, my friend, you're not the only one here who hates their life. Most of the time I wish I were dead, but I think God keeps me alive just for spite. Nobody should suffer like this."

Elaine related to Jessie's pain. She was just about to comfort her when Jessie stormed out of the room and ran down the hallway. Elaine followed her and pushed open the door that Jessie had so forcefully slammed.

Jessie stood by her window and knelt down. When Elaine realized Jessie was praying, she patiently waited by the door until she was finished. Then Elaine asked the inevitable. "Why didn't you tell me about any of this? Why did you tell me your son was alive?"

"Because I was ashamed. I wanted to tell you, really I did, but I just couldn't."

"Didn't you think I would understand?"

"I don't know what I was thinking. Can you forgive me?" Jessie asked with concern.

"Of course. I know you didn't mean to lie to me. I know it's difficult to talk about certain things."

"Does that mean you're not mad at me?" Jessie asked with optimism in her voice.

"Exactly," Elaine said as she took hold of Jessie and gave her a hug. "We're friends and sometimes we do things that shouldn't have to be explained. This was just one of them. So let's forget all about this. If that's okay with you?"

Jessie nodded her head in appreciation.

***

Jessie was late for breakfast the next morning. By the time she had gotten to the dining room, Elaine had finished both of their breakfasts.

"Boy, you were hungry today," Jessie said as she sat down beside Elaine. "I'm glad someone has an appetite today, 'cause I'm sure not hungry."

Elaine couldn't help but notice Jessie's red, swollen eyes. She debated whether or not to ask Jessie about them, but decided against it. She already knew the answer.

Elaine tried to skillfully shift Jessie into better spirits. "The food is either getting much better or I was hungrier than I thought."

"The food tastes like shit," Jessie said as she pawned a piece of bacon from someone else's plate. "But if you're hungry, you eat."

Then, from out of the blue, Jessie asked Elaine in a very forthright manner, "What did you do to escape your pain?"

Elaine, who by now had learned to honestly answer questions, responded quickly. "I went to the racetrack."

Jessie seemed surprised. "The racetrack?" she asked. "You've never mentioned the racetrack.

"Yes, the racetrack. When I was at the track, the only thing that mattered was what horse I picked. It was all so simple.

"Did you lose a lot of money?"

"No. As a matter of fact, I was very lucky. I won most of the time and, to be perfectly honest with you, I didn't care if I won or lost. All that mattered was my mind could rest. I didn't worry or care about anything. I was totally free and that felt good. Very good."

"I can understand that," Jessie said as she stood up. "Are you ready to get out of here?" she asked Elaine.

"Where to?"

"I don't know. How about a walk?"

"Sounds good to me," Elaine responded quickly.

After their walk, Jessie lingered in the garden for a long time, losing all track of time. Once again, Jessie had missed lunch.

Mary stood behind Elaine and whispered in her ear, "Have you seen Jessie today?"

Elaine nodded as she turned around and said, "Yes, we went walking for a long time today. What's wrong?"

Mary's eyes filled with concern. "Oh, nothing. I was just wondering if you might check the garden for me. Jessie loves that garden. That's where she goes to do her thinking. I thought being with a friend might help."

Mary didn't have to say another word. Elaine was on her way to find Jessie. When Elaine first approached, Jessie didn't say anything. But she did join her on the grass.

"I'm glad you're here," Jessie said as she tried to force a smile. "I haven't been able to sleep, which is pretty weird, because when I first got here that's all I did. That's how I escaped. All I did was sleep. I never ate or got out of bed. In fact, for a while they had to feed me intravenously, but I used to yank out the needle."

Jessie stopped talking for a private moment, reminding herself of her early days at the Pavilion.

"I practically starved myself to death. If it weren't for Mary's help, I probably would have died. She's a terrific nurse and she's been a good friend, but I wish she hadn't been so caring. I would have probably died and that really would have been a blessing."

Elaine interrupted. "I don't think so. If that had been the case, we never would have met."

"I'm really very tired," Jessie said as she stood up. "Will you walk me back to my room? My legs are a little wobbly. I think I'll take a nap.

Elaine did as she asked.

∗∗∗

In the days that followed, Elaine began to notice that Jessie was acting quite differently. Dark shadows had deepened under her eyes, exhibiting her lack of sleep, and Jessie's spirited conversation had seemed to cease as the days passed. Even their walks had dwindled, and late at night, Elaine once again watched TV alone. Something was very wrong with Jessie.

The next morning, instead of wondering if Jessie would join her and the others for breakfast, Elaine walked down to her room. After three knocks with no response, Elaine opened the door, calling out, "Jess, are you in there?"

Elaine opened the bathroom door, only to find a spotless room without even a tube of toothpaste on the counter. Thinking how strange this was, Elaine walked down to the nursing station, looking for Mary.

By now, Elaine was feeling quite anxious, so she jumped when Mary surfaced from behind and tapped her shoulder. "Oh, it's you Mary," Elaine said as she took a deep breath. "You scared me."

When she looked into Mary's eyes, Elaine was certain something very bad had happened.

Mary spoke softer than usual. "Dr. Caufield would like to see you in his office."

Elaine's heart was beating overtime as she ran down the hall into Ben's office. She didn't knock, she just entered.

Elaine had never remembered seeing such sadness in Ben's eyes.

"What's wrong? What's happened?" Elaine's voice had become desperate.

Ben took his time in answering. "Elaine, please have a seat," he said as he motioned for her to sit.

"I don't want to sit," Elaine said with a thunderous tone. "What's going on here? What's happened to Jessie? Is she sick?"

As Ben spoke, he stood up and walked toward Elaine. "I'm afraid it's much worse than that."

Elaine's face grew pale and her eyes filled with tears. "What could be worse than that?" By that time, the message became clear. "Oh my God, what happened?" she cried out.

"We lost her last night," Ben said with astonishing compassion. "Her heart gave out."

"I don't believe you," Elaine shouted out. "You're not going to tell me the truth, are you? She tried to kill herself, didn't she?"

Ben sat beside Elaine, reaching for her hand, but Elaine pushed him away. "Why are you lying to me? Jessie wasn't sick. She would have told me."

Mary's calming voice interrupted. "She wanted to, but she decided against it. I explained to her you would understand and would rather hear it from her, but she didn't want to alarm you. She had serious heart problems."

Still in disbelief, Elaine shouted out, "She killed herself, didn't she? Didn't she? Damn it, she was too young to die. You're lying to me."

Once again, Ben tried to comfort Elaine. "If you get nothing else out of our sessions, you will understand that I don't lie. I believe lies are destructive. So please believe me. Jessie did not commit suicide. She just stopped trying."

Elaine looked over at Mary. Mary nodded her head in agreement.

Before going back to her room, Elaine turned back to look at the two of them and said, "Sometimes life is too damn hard."

Chapter 22

With concern, Ben approved Elaine's decision to attend Jessie's funeral. He did so hoping that somewhere between the pain and the uncertainty, good would prevail. He was right.

Nothing really changed at first. Elaine would come to her therapy sessions with absolutely nothing to discuss. She would sit down, say hello and that was that. No conversation or tears.

Ben wasn't the least bit phased by her demeanor. He had seen her that way before, and his confidence in human nature left room for Elaine's transformation. Her attitude didn't scare him. It only made him work that much harder.

Occasionally, he would ask Elaine a question or two, but she rarely answered. Once again, the silence lingered.

It was during a morning session when the first ray of sunshine came through at last. Elaine asked if it would be possible to read a page from her diary.

Ben was delighted that she would allow him to be a part of her private world, definitely a positive action.

Elaine pulled a small, brown diary from her bag. She reached inside for the key, opened the book and started to read.

To my dearest diary:

I haven't written for days because I had very little to say. One of the kindest friends I've ever had died. We understood each other, even when we didn't talk. We used to laugh, as we referred to each other as one half of a pair of shoes that needed to be fixed.

At first I didn't believe anyone about her death. They said Jessie's heart gave out, but I wasn't listening. Truthfully, I didn't care why, I just cared that it happened. Jessie was dead and nothing could bring her back. I thought she killed herself. Why not? I tried, but Jessie wasn't as horrible as I was. I tried to kill myself, but my unborn baby died instead. I can't go back, but I can go forward.

It's time to make a choice. I can stay here at the Castleberry and live in what I thought was the perfect world, where nothing bad ever happens, or rejoin the world I left. If I stay here, I will only have a past. I need a future. I would like to give back some of the time I have taken from Martin. It's time to join the living. I think if the shoemaker can only fix one of the shoes, the other should stand alone. After all, there are people out there with only one leg. If they can do it, so can I.

Elaine

"So what do you think?" Elaine said as she closed her diary. "Do you think Martin could come here to see me? That is, if he wants to."

Ben eased back against his chair and smiled. "Do I think Martin will come, you ask? Absolutely. I don't think there's anything he would rather do. Are you sure?" Ben repeated, just to set the record straight.

"Yes, very sure."

"Good. Then I'll arrange for a visit."

***

The receptionist at the Castleberry greeted Martin in a friendly manner.

"Good afternoon. Can I be of assistance?" she asked.

"Yes, thank you. Ben Caufield is expecting me. I'm Martin Lewis," Martin politely answered with an anxious voice.

"The doctor's office is straight down the hall and two doors to the right."

Martin bowed his head in appreciation.

As he walked down the hall, Martin's thoughts filtered back to his first full day at the Meridian Hospital and how tense and awkward he had felt. Right at that moment, he felt like the young intern who doubted himself.

He knocked on Ben's door.

"Come in," Ben said as he stood up and walked toward the door.

First came the handshake, then the long-overdue hug.

"Ben, I don't know what to say."

Laughing just a bit, Ben looked at his old friend. "I can't believe the most talkative medical student I ever knew is at a loss for words."

The ice was broken and comfort set in. Martin smiled and said, "I've waited for this day for so long, now that I'm here I'm so dammed nervous I'm ready to turn around and run like hell."

"But you won't," Ben added.

"You're right, I won't," Martin said with commitment. "I love her too much. How is she? Really."

Ben motioned for Martin to have a seat. "Actually, she's been making steady progress over the last few weeks."

"Do you think she's ready to see me?" Martin asked with concern. "You can tell me what you think. At this point you don't have to coat the truth. Don't worry, I'm a lot stronger than I was."

"As a matter of fact, I do think she's ready. But enough about what I think. Why don't you go see for yourself?" Ben added as he looked down at his watch. "She's in the garden."

"Garden?" Martin questioned. "Elaine was never much of an outdoor person."

Ben smiled. "Well, she is now. The garden has been very comforting to her. It's the place she goes to when she wants to think things out. Several of my patients find consolation out there. And, if I must confess, so do I."

Suddenly, a worried look appeared on Martin's face. "Do you think in all her changing she has fallen out of love with me?"

"No, I don't. I think you're really going to like what you see."

Martin stood up. He took a long, cleansing, deep breath and walked toward the door. "I know I'm going to like what I see, but will she?"

No answer was necessary.

***

Elaine didn't notice Martin watching her. He stood in silence, watching her every move and knowing without a doubt he loved her more than ever.

Finally, after several long moments of Martin wondering just how he would approach Elaine, she turned around.

Her eyes magnetically held his stare. A tear or two trickled down her face. She smiled and, without speaking a word, she had his full attention.

It was several minutes before either of them spoke. With deliberate, uniform steps, they walked toward each other. In the silence of the moment, Elaine was once again in Martin's arms.

"You're as beautiful as ever," Martin whispered to her.

"Do you really think so?" she asked, deliberately holding back her tears.

Martin's smile was convincing. "Yes I do, but I've always thought that."

With soft, gentle motions, Elaine's trembling fingers stroked Martin's hair. "You're still the kindest man I know."

Elaine had not anticipated her own eager response to Martin's lips. She was completely caught off-guard by the way she felt when he kissed her.

Elaine reached for Martin's hand as she directed him toward the bench she had been seated on before he arrived.

"Look at what I'm wearing," she said as she pointed to the diamond heart necklace positioned ever so elegantly on her neck.

Martin's eyes widened in surprise. "Oh my, I haven't seen that necklace in years."

"I haven't worn it in years."

Martin couldn't help but ask the obvious. "How on earth did it get here?"

Elaine was rather proud of her reasoning. "I've had it in an envelope for years. I kept it in a very safe place, just in case the day would come when I would want to wear it again. Today is that day."

"I remember exactly when I gave it to you," Martin added in remembrance. "It was on our first anniversary, right after your second chocolate mousse.

Elaine smiled. "You do remember, don't you?"

"There is very little about you I don't remember," Martin said with pride.

They walked for a long while before either of them spoke. Within the quietness of their thoughts came memories.

Martin had managed to keep his attention on the moment instead of recalling anything that might be construed as unpleasant.

Elaine, who knew Martin's plan exactly, thrashed several of her own remembrances around in her mind. When she couldn't seem to keep them to herself, she bellowed out, "You know, despite what you might think, I do love Stevie. I always have."

Martin stopped dead in his tracks. He couldn't believe what he had just heard. He didn't know exactly how to respond to such an outburst.

Martin felt a little unsteady, but kept it to himself. When they approached a bench, he decided it would be best if he sat down for awhile. He hadn't expected Elaine to bring up Stevie at all, let alone so early in their first visit.

Elaine joined him on the bench. She reached for his hand and held on tightly. "One of the things I've learned here is to say what's on my mind, so please understand. I realize you are not used to me being this open. You remember me doing just the opposite. I was very good at hiding the truth."

"Yes, I know," Martin added, accepting this kind of behavior as healthy. "Did you want to talk about this some more?" he asked, anxious to do the right thing.

Elaine was quick to answer. "Not today, but I just wanted you to know."

Martin nodded, sympathetic to her decision.

***

Later, just as Martin was about to leave, Elaine said, "Goodbye" in a rather innocent tone and then kissed Martin's cheek. "Thank you for coming."

Martin, who had been all too eager to take her in his arms and beg her to come home with him, didn't. He held her very tightly and didn't let go for several minutes. "I have somewhat of a confession to make," he said as he removed his arms from her waist.

"A confession?" Elaine asked. "Go on, I'm listening."

"Remember the day we met?" he asked, not certain that she did.

"Of course I do."

"Well, I was finishing up my rounds in the hospital that day when I noticed you sitting in the hospital lobby. I couldn't help but notice you. You were so very beautiful. I had this feeling in the pit of my stomach that you were the woman I had dreamt about. The woman I would marry. I just had to figure out how to meet you."

By this time, Elaine's face turned a rose color. "How could you have known that?" she asked, amazed at his confession.

"Some things you just know. This was one of them. Well, anyway, as long as I started, I might as well finish."

"Fine. I'm listening."

"Then, if you remember, I dropped my stethoscope."

Elaine smirked. "Yes. As a matter of fact, I do remember that."

"I was just killing time, trying to think of a nonchalant way of asking you to join me for a cup of coffee."

"That's when I asked you if you would like a cup of coffee," Elaine also confessed to the memory.

"But I knew the coffee shop was already closed for the day," Martin added.

"Me, too," Elaine conceded.

Martin seemed surprised. "You did? How come you never told me that before?"

"It never came up in conversation. I was also hoping you would invite me to dinner."

"But I did."

"I know, and I was very glad you did. The rest is history," Elaine added on a up note.

"Is that what we have, a history?"

"I hope so," Elaine concluded.

"Me too," Martin said as he held Elaine's hand and gave it a proper squeeze.

Chapter 23

That evening, Ben arranged an extra session for Elaine. Even before he asked any questions, Ben could sense that Martin's visit was a success.

"Looks like today's encounter went pretty well. Am I right?" Ben asked with assurance.

"How can you tell?"

"That's my job. Besides, you're a dead give away. You're wearing makeup and, to go along with the lipstick you're wearing, you have a smile on your face."

Elaine sat back in her chair and lifted her hands over her head, bridging her fingers in a relaxed manner. "As a matter of fact, I really do feel pretty dammed good."

Relief appeared on Ben's face. "I'm glad."

"I don't know if you're planning to ask me if I said anything significant to Martin, but I'll tell you. I told him I loved Stevie."

"Did you have an extensive conversation?" Ben asked with concern.

"No, not really. I don't think I'm ready. Do you?"

"You'll know when you are," Ben added.

***

The very moment Martin stepped into his doorway, Maggie called out to him, "I'll be right there."

"You look like you had a good day," Maggie said as she helped Martin off with his coat.

"I most certainly did. I actually felt closer to Elaine than ever before."

A satisfactory smile appeared on Maggie's face. "Well good for you."

"She was like a different person. She was a lot more open than she had been in the past. She even admitted to loving Stevie."

"Now that is good news. When will she be coming home?" Maggie asked.

"We never got that far. I spoke to the doctor briefly before I left and we decided we'd take one day at a time, especially with Elaine's sensitivity. I don't want to pressure her at all."

Maggie's face invoked pleasure. "Pretty soon, if God is good, you'll be a family."

Martin smiled. "From your mouth to God's ears."

"Oh, by the way," Maggie added. "Mrs. Braverman called several times."

"Thanks," Martin said as he reached for the telephone.

"Sal, it's Martin. I know I promised to call you from the Castleberry, but I was so happy about how well the day went, I forgot."

On the other end, Sally listened as Martin went on and on about Elaine. She couldn't seem to get a word in edgewise until Martin was just about to hang up.

"Sal, that just about does it for today's visit. I really appreciate you just listening. Sometimes I go on and on, especially when I'm overtired and very anxious. I guess today I'm a little of both."

"Martin," Sally paused for a moment, wondering if she should go on with her request or just say goodbye. But she asked anyway. "Do you think it would be possible to see Elaine? I really do miss her quite a bit."

"That would really be nice, but I'll have to ask Ben."

"Thanks hon, I really think it would be a good idea. Sometimes a girl needs a friend," Sally said right before she hung up.

***

Ben Caufield approved the idea of Sally visiting Elaine.

Sally had stopped three times on the way there. First she picked up Elaine's favorite candies, then a couple bags of pretzels and then, last but not least, a pack of cigarettes, hoping things wouldn't go badly enough to make her smoke. But Sally always prepared herself for any sort of distraction.

Sally did concise yoga breathing before she opened the car door to get out. She surprised herself for even remembering one stress reliever, but after forty or fifty sessions, something should have stuck in her head.

Ben Caufield was quite a bit more charming than she had imagined. She would tell Martin that if there ever came a time when she needed a place like the Castleberry, to make the arrangements for Ben Caufield to aid in her recovery.

"Hello," Sally said as she held out her hand to greet Ben. "Thank you for allowing me time to see Elaine. I miss her."

After a strong handshake, Ben escorted Sally to sit down. "She's missed you. She's spoken of you during several of our sessions."

Sally's face flushed. "Oh, I see. I hope it was all good and not too revealing."

"Not to worry," Ben said while smiling. "It was only surface."

Sally gave a relieved smile. "Well, that's good." She paused for a moment. "At least I hope that's good."

"Elaine is waiting for you in her room," Ben said. "She's been looking forward to seeing you."

"How long can I stay?"

"No limit, unless there's a problem, which I'm sure there won't be."

"Thanks for your vote of confidence, Dr. Caufield."

"Call me Ben, please. Most of my patients do."

"What about your friends?" Sally added with a laugh.

"Oh, my friends. Well, they call me Dr. Caufield." Then he smiled, revealing that he also had a sense of humor.

"Goodbye Ben," Sally said as she walked out of his office with impressively sexy sways, certain Ben was watching.

She was right. He was.

***

Sally knocked twice and then walked into Elaine's room, expecting to see a fragile and feminine Elaine. Instead, she was greeted by a much stronger and healthier young woman.

Elaine's eyes were more blue and clear than before and her short, wavy hair had grown. She now wore it down smoothly, with gentle waves around her hairline. Her face, which had always lacked color, now had a healthy glow. All and all, Elaine was more beautiful than Sally had remembered.

Elaine ran to Sally and embraced her. "You don't know how glad I am to see you," Elaine said, meaning every word.

"If you would have called for me sooner I would have been here," Sally explained.

Elaine smiled. "I know that. I really wasn't very comfortable talking with anyone outside of here. In fact, for a long time I didn't want to speak to anyone here, even Ben."

Sally turned on a smile. "Now he's a pretty damn cute one. I wouldn't mind talking to him about anything."

Elaine gave Sally a hug. "It's nice to see some things never change."

Am I that boring?" Sally asked.

"No. You're that interesting," Elaine said with conviction. "It's just nice to see someone you can count on."

"That's me, dependable. Just like an old watch," Sally said, half-kidding. "So tell me how you really are."

"Better. Much better," Elaine explained.

"Can I sit?" Sally asked as she pointed to the chair by the window.

"Of course. I'm sorry. My social graces are a little bit rusty."

"Not to worry. I hope you're feeling as good as you look."

"To be honest with you, I really am feeling much better. There were days when I thought getting better would be impossible, but now it's going to happen. I know it is."

"Me too," Sally added.

Sally kept her eye on Elaine at all times, making sure their conversation didn't get too tense. Sally was afraid to question Elaine, but she went ahead and asked anyway. "Why didn't you let me help you?"

"Because you couldn't. No one could. It was me."

"I would have tried," Sally continued. "Maybe I could have steered you away from Josh." Right at that moment Sally stopped herself, embarrassed for going a bit too far.

Elaine noticed the delay in Sally's conversation. "That's okay. I won't crack. Not anymore. We can talk about Josh if you want to," Elaine said, not bothered by the situation.

"I don't think he's worth talking about," Sally said with a great sense of conviction.

Elaine couldn't help but wonder about his life after her attempted suicide. "I really feel badly about bringing Josh into my nightmare."

"Don't worry too much about Josh Derman. He's a fighter. Men like Josh Derman survive."

"I hope so," Elaine added in a sympathetic tone.

"I don't think I can ever see Josh again, but I must say some things to him that only I can say. Maybe I should call him."

"What about a letter?" Sally suggested.

"A letter? I don't know. Maybe that's a little too impersonal."

"Not really. Seeing him right now is probably not in your best interest. Why don't you let it go for awhile?"

"I can't do that. But I will send him a letter. The day may come when I do more. For now, that's the best I can do."

When Sally didn't respond, Elaine knew why.

***

The following day, Elaine compromised with her decision. She sent Josh a telegram.

Josh was in bed when the doorbell rang. Of course, he was not alone. A long-legged blonde lay next to him. She had a beautiful smile and a lovely voice, but if anyone were to ask Josh her last name, he wouldn't know it. Such was the case with most of his bed partners.

When he wasn't kidding himself, Josh thought about Elaine. But it wasn't until that night that he realized just how much she had meant to him.

By the time he had gotten to the door, the messenger was gone, but the telegram was under his apartment door.

He sat on the couch and read.

Dear Josh,

I don't really know where to begin, so I think I'll start with a simple thank you. I know it was you who saved my life and I will be forever grateful.

For the last several months, if you had asked me if I wanted to live, I might have answered with a definite no. But now that I am feeling better, I am very glad I didn't die.

I haven't discussed that night with anyone, but if it hadn't been for you, I would have been alone. And then my life would have been over.

I often wonder what would have happened had I not been so sad when we met and things would have been different. I guess neither of us will ever know the answer to that question.

You made me smile when I had no reason to. I can still remember your jokes and the way you made me laugh. I don't think anyone else could have or ever will have that effect on me.

If I've caused you any pain, I am really very sorry. If you're wondering why I am not saying this to you in person, it is because I can't, at least not yet.

The right woman will be out there somewhere. She will be the lucky one.

Once again, I thank you for your love. I will never forget you.

Love, Elaine

For a very long time, Josh sat on the couch in silence, clenching the telegram to his chest. Closing his eyes, he reminded himself of Elaine's beautiful face and of her gracious innocence.

He didn't expect to feel as disappointed as he was. Although he was pleased to hear of her recovery, he felt a loss beyond tears.

Walking slowly back to his bed, he subconsciously felt Elaine's presence.

But in reality, once he reached the foot of his bed, there lay the same blonde who had been there earlier. He wanted to tell her to leave, but he didn't.

It didn't really matter if she stayed the night or not, tomorrow he would have forgotten her face.

Josh knew that true love only came once. He had lost his chance, but he would always remember Elaine's beautiful face. Some things could never be forgotten.

Chapter 24

Ben had just given Elaine the news. In his estimation, she was ready to leave the Castleberry. However, it was ultimately up to her. Ben guided, but never pushed.

Mary was waiting for Elaine when she got back to her room. "Did you hear the news?" Elaine asked as she sat down on the edge of her bed and crisscrossed her legs.

Mary watched in amazement. "Every time I see you do that, I wish I could."

Elaine patted her bed, offering Mary a seat. "I'll teach you."

"Thanks, but no thanks. I'm not as flexible as you are. And yes, I heard the good news."

At that moment, the conversation took on a serious note.

"I'm scared," Elaine confessed. "What if I'm really not ready to leave? I'm comfortable here. I have you and the good doctor to keep me on my toes. What if I fail?"

Mary took Elaine up on her idea and took a seat on the bed beside her. "We've known each other for awhile, so I hope you'll understand what I'm going to say to you is in good faith and with your best interest in mind."

Elaine nodded.

"You've made mistakes. God knows we've all made them, but there comes a time when you have to let go. I think that time is now. God forgives."

Elaine's eyes filled with tears. "I don't think my sins can ever be forgotten."

"I didn't say forgotten. I said forgiven. Even if you can't forget the things you did, you can still go on living. It's fine to remember the past, but it won't do you any good to stay in it. You're a young woman. You have a husband who loves you and a son who needs you."

"A son. Yes, that's right, I have a son."

Mary was joyous. "Did you hear yourself?" she asked Elaine. "You said you had a son."

Elaine was startled by her own words. "You're right. I did say that, didn't I?"

"I rest my case," Mary added.

The beginning of a smile tipped the corners of Elaine's mouth.

***

The time had been set. Martin would pick Elaine up before noon the next day.

The afternoon before Elaine's departure from the Castleberry, Martin found himself driving around endlessly. He had long awaited Elaine's arrival but, as the final hours approached, he was sleepless and overanxious.

He had phoned his mother to tell her the news, completely forgetting she was on another cruise. Sometimes he felt years older, and certainly a bit more stuffy, than his mother. She was always ready for action. Another trip, another play, a dance, whatever, Esther was on her way.

After stopping at two or three fast-food chains, Martin grew tired of eating. His nerves were again playing tricks on him. How many hamburgers and fries could any man have?

Sally was out and Cecil was involved in a new surgical procedure at the hospital. Martin was once again alone. He needed Stevie.

He looked at his watch. It was after five. If he didn't hit too much traffic, he might be able to take Stevie to dinner. Stevie would be happy and so would he.

Martin rang the doorbell.

Sophie, drying off her hands with her apron, opened the door. "Why, Doctor, what a surprise. Please come in."

"I'm really sorry to barge in this way," Martin said, flustered. "But I was wondering if it would be possible for Stevie to have dinner with me."

Sophie was charmed. "Of course he can. Doctor, you know whenever you want to see Stevie, it's alright with me."

"I just thought dinner time and all..."

Sophie interrupted. "Would you like to have dinner with us?"

"Thank you, but as long as I'm here, I know how much Stevie loves pizza. So pizza it is."

Sophie nodded. "I'll be right back. I'll get him."

"Thanks," Martin said as he sat down on the couch. He cracked his fingers nervously, trying to occupy his mind with idle thoughts. It wasn't working, but at least he was trying.

Then, faster than a speeding bullet, Stevie came running down the stairs shouting, "Daddy, Daddy."

Stevie embraced Martin in one of his active but tender hugs. Immediately, Martin felt at ease and certainly content with his decision to see Stevie, the prescription of choice.

Chapter 25

It was seven in the morning. Maggie glanced over at the wall clock. To double check the time, she walked into Martin's study and again looked at the clock. It was now five after seven.

Martin was usually on his second cup of coffee by now. Because it was such a special day, Maggie assumed he would have been up and dressed by five. That wouldn't have surprised her. But when he wasn't up at seven, that puzzled her.

As she walked up the stairs, her heart was beating rapidly. She was alarmed and she didn't know why.

As she reached the top of the stairs, she heard a loud thud coming from Martin's bedroom. She panicked, but knocked before going in.

There was no answer. She quickly ran to where Martin had fallen to the floor. He was tightly grasping a small bottle of pills. The pills were scattered all over the floor as he lay motionless.

"Oh my God, Martin, what has happened?" she cried out. "Please God, don't let this happen."

Maggie's hands were trembling as she reached for the phone. "Please come, we have an emergency at 369 Green Bay Road... Dr. Martin Lewis.... hurry..."

***

Elaine sat in the hospital, praying for a miracle. This wasn't exactly the homecoming she had expected. But then again, her entire life had not exactly been any young girl's dream.

It was difficult for her to watch Martin lying there — with tubes, wires, and other mechanical devices giving him life — without blaming herself.

Sally stood silently, rubbing Elaine's shoulders and sighing in exhaustion. "It might be a good idea to take a break. Maybe a cup of coffee or something like that."

Elaine shook her head. "No thanks. You go. I want to be here when Martin wakes up."

Sally slowly released her hands from Elaine's shoulders. She leaned down and whispered in Elaine's ear, "Come on, hon, just for a short while. This has been a long day for you."

Elaine turned around and, in an agitated voice, spoke out. "A long day for me? What about Martin? It's been a long day for him. What if he wakes up and no one's here? Then what? What if Martin is frightened?"

"We won't be gone long," Sally explained. "I just don't want you to overdo it."

"For the first time in our married life, I want to be here for Martin, whatever it takes. He's always been there for me. Don't you think it's about time?" Elaine disputed.

Sally recognized defeat. "Okay, if you insist, but I'm going to bring you back a cup of coffee whether you like it or not. I won't take no for an answer."

Elaine turned around and looked at Sally, who was all teary eyed. "I'm sorry. Forgive me. I would appreciate it if you would bring me back a cup of coffee. It does sound good. I'm just very nervous, so please don't pay attention to me."

"I know that," Sally confessed. "Me too."

"Sal, before you go, can I ask you something?"

"Sure, what is it?"

"Why didn't Martin tell me?"

"He didn't want to upset you."

"How long has he had a heart condition?"

Sally acknowledged Elaine's fears. "For a while, but he always said it wasn't serious. He referred to his condition as no big deal. If he takes his pills, he's okay. If he doesn't, well, now we're here."

When Sally was out of sight, Elaine pushed her chair even closer to Martin's bed. With gentle movements, she stroked Martin's forehead. She spoke very softly to him. "I love you, Martin. Please forgive me for being so dammed selfish. Now that I'm home, everything's going to be different. You'll see I've changed."

When Sally returned, Elaine was seated outside Martin's room. "What's going on? Why are you out here?" Sally asked as she placed the coffee cup on the table beside Elaine.

"Changing of shifts. New nurses, which means temperature, blood pressure, and whatever. Some of the nurses stretch the rules a bit and let me stay in his room, but others go exactly by the book. They'll call me when I can go back in."

Sally nodded in approval. "Maybe you should ask if there's an extra cot for you to sleep on. You need your rest."

"And what about you?" Elaine asked Sally as she motioned to join her on the couch.

"If it's me you're worrying about, forget it. I'm here for however long it takes. Don't forget, I've known Martin since we were kids. I can't leave the ship. Not now."

Elaine nodded and smiled briefly, reminding herself of how lucky she and Martin had been to have a friend as wonderful as Sally. That was the last time Elaine mentioned anything to Sally about leaving. If anyone should be there, it was Sally.

***

It was early afternoon. Elaine had been wiping Martin's brow when she felt him twinge. At first she thought it was her imagination, but a moment later, Martin opened his eyes. He didn't speak, but she was certain there had been some movement.

She quickly buzzed for a nurse and yelled into the speaker, "It's my husband. I think he's waking."

Several nurses ran in. Elaine moved out of their way, making herself almost invisible.

Her heart pounded as she watched Martin slowly coming to. Not only was he breathing on his own, but his color had started to return. Elaine gave a sigh of relief.

"Mrs. Lewis," one of the nurses called over to where she had been standing. "Could you please have a seat outside for a few minutes?"

"Okay, if I have to," Elaine said, hesitant to oblige. "Before I leave, can I say something to my husband?"

"Yes," the nurse agreed. "But I don't think he'll remember anything you say now."

"That's okay."

Elaine walked over to Martin's bed and reached for his hand. "Martin, it's me, Elaine. I'm here with you, but for now they want me outside. Don't worry about a thing. You're going to be just fine."

Elaine joined Sally in the waiting room. They both paced back and forth like soldiers on assignment. Every minute seemed like an eternity.

Finally, one of the nurses came out of Martin's room and walked over. She looked at Elaine and, with delight, pointed to Martin's room. "There's someone quite anxious to see you in there."

Sally hugged Elaine while smiling with relief. "Never let a man like Martin wait. Go for it," Sally added. "I'll be out here if you need me."

"You're the best," Elaine said as she once again embraced Sally.

Elaine dashed into Martin's room, too nervous to speak. She composed herself as best she could and then, despite all the wires and tubes that were attached to Martin, she kissed his forehead and said, "You can't imagine how worried I was."

Martin's voice was just a fraction above a whisper. "I'm sorry I couldn't be there to take you home. I wanted your homecoming to be special."

Tears filled Elaine's eyes as she spoke. "Martin, I can't believe it. After all you've been through, you're apologizing to me? You really are something."

"No, not really. I just love you."

***

Sally finally agreed to go home, but Elaine refused to leave Martin's side. She sat for hours at a time, watching him fall in and out of sleep. He occasionally spoke, but most of the time they gazed into each other's eyes, expressing a silent sadness. Each reminding themselves of the secret they kept from each another.

Elaine wondered if Martin also regretted the time that was lost. Elaine spoke to him about her mistakes, wondering if he would remember her words. She didn't care if he did, but at least she felt better airing out some of her bad feelings.

Time was passing quickly. Doctors, doctors and more doctors. Martin had been tested and poked at for days; he was a human pincushion. Finally, the verdict was in — open-heart surgery was the only way to go.

"Are you afraid?" Elaine asked Martin the first moment they were alone.

"Yes, but I'm not surprised. It was inevitable. I knew I was on borrowed time. I was just hoping Stevie would be a little older when I had the surgery, and maybe he wouldn't need me so much."

"You're not going to die," Elaine cried out.

"I know that. But Stevie won't understand any of this. He's used to me visiting him. He'll be lonely, but he won't understand why."

"Martin, I'm really so sorry about all this. I wish I could take back all those horrible years. I don't know what to do. How to make it up to you. There are so many new adjustments that have to be made. I hope I can handle all of this, but I don't know if I can."

Martin reached for Elaine's hand. "You can."

"How can you be so sure?" Elaine asked with extreme concern. "This is all so new to me. Maybe I'll disappoint you."

"You won't. I know you won't. We're going to pull our lives together. You'll see this can work. I know it will."

Elaine continued to hold a vigilant watch. Martin seemed unable to rest properly. He seemed distracted and uneasy.

Elaine felt it necessary to confront him. "What's going on? Something is very wrong. You don't have to be afraid. If we're ever going to make it, we have to be able to say what's on our minds. So please, go ahead and tell me. No more secrets."

Martin struggled within his mind, deciding if he should ask Elaine what he knew he must. Finally, he just came right out and asked. "Will you see Stevie for me? Please."

Elaine's face turned as white as a ghost. "Martin, I can't do that, not yet. I'm afraid. I'm not ready. No, not yet," she begged. "I want to be able to go there with you. I can't go alone. When you get well, we'll go there together. I won't know what to say. I won't know what to do."

***

Elaine might not have known what to do or say, but she did go. The very next day, she paced back and forth in front of Sophie's house. It wasn't going to be easy, but the hard part was over. She was there. It was time to grow up and be the woman both Martin and Stevie needed..

She took several deep breaths before knocking. Right after her last knock, the panic really set in. Her heart was beating so fast she could hardly breathe.

She was just about to turn and walk away when the door opened. Elaine remembered Sophie's face as clear as if it had been yesterday when Stevie left the hospital in her arms.

Sophie graciously smiled as she said, "Come in."

Elaine smiled back. "I'm really sorry I'm so late. I was just so nervous. I wasn't sure I could make it at all."

"I understand," Sophie told her as she led Elaine into the living room.

Elaine sat down on the sofa by the wall. Two cups of tea and some sweets were placed before her. Elaine desperately hoped she could be courteous when the tea was offered to her. Food would be inappropriate for Elaine's threat of queasiness. Sophie sat beside Elaine and immediately poured the tea. Elaine nodded in acceptance.

Sophie was a little nervous herself, indicated by her unsteady hand as she filled the teacups. Elaine politely took a sip, but just one. It was all she could handle.

After a long pause in their informal conversation, Elaine spoke up. "You must think I'm horrible. You have raised my son for me because I have shirked my duties as a mother. I abandoned my own son. I can only imagine what shallow opinion of me you must have."

"I have never thought of you in that way at all. Believe me, I rarely, if ever, make any judgment on someone I do not know," Sophie remarked. "You did what you had to."

Elaine looked at Sophie, wondering when the bomb would drop. Elaine couldn't imagine that the woman who sat beside her could think anything but dreadful thoughts about her. Completely apropos, she imagined.

Sophie quietly sipped the tea. "May I call you Elaine?" she respectfully asked.

"Of course."

"Well then, Elaine, please have some tea. It will ease your nerves."

"I don't think anything can ease my nerves today."

Sophie smiled at Elaine. "Then let me help you. Take a few deep breaths and you'll be fine."

Elaine recognized her kindness. "Thank you for trying to help, but I've already tried that. I'm just so jumpy today."

"You're going to be fine," Sophie reassured her. "You have a wonderful son and believe me, with a boy like Stevie, you won't have to worry about a thing. He'll help you. He's very gentle and giving."

Elaine resented sitting there, allowing some woman she barely knew to tell her about how wonderful her son was.

While Sophie talked, Elaine scanned the room with her eyes. It was filled with photos and ribbons symbolizing the children's awards. Suddenly Elaine felt embarrassed by her doubts. Sophie obviously cared a great deal about all the children who lived with her.

Sophie picked up on Elaine's doubts. "Aren't they wonderful pictures?" she asked. "My kids are my life, and let me tell you something, they're the greatest bunch of kids I've ever had."

Elaine now felt foolish for doubting Sophie. Here sat a woman who clearly loved each and every one of her children in a very special way. It was they who were lucky.

That was when Elaine decided it was a horrible mistake for her to be there. That's when she headed for the door.

"Sophie, you've been very hospitable, but I think it would be better if I leave now. This visit was a mistake. I'm sorry if I've caused you any trouble," Elaine said in an apologetic voice.

"You haven't caused me any trouble. Please don't go. Elaine, you've come so far across the board, why don't you follow through with your plan? I don't think you'll be sorry."

"Plans change, life changes. The world is filled with changes, broken promises, and lies. If I walked out the door and never came back, who would know the difference?"

Sophie spoke with challenge in her voice when she interrupted Elaine. "You would know the difference. You would be missing the best part of your life. Stevie is your flesh and blood. You're his mother. You gave him life. Why not give him love?"

Right at that moment, Elaine felt anger rush through her body. She was furious. She shouted in anger. "What do you know about how I feel? You couldn't possibly know what I'm feeling. No one could."

"Oh, but I do know. Only too well," Sophie said, clarifying her position. "My first born was severely handicapped. Robbie was far more developmentally handicapped than Stevie. I couldn't even say his name out loud for at least a year. I refused to see him. I swore I'd never look into his eyes. After all, how could I? I was the one who caused him such pain. It was my fault and there was no telling me any different.

"Then one day, everything changed. Robbie needed surgery. The home Robbie lived in called me. They didn't think he would live through the night, but he did. From that moment on, instead of my son being the worst part of my life, he was the very best. Up until his very last breath, I was never sorry I had given him love."

Elaine just stood there in shock. "I don't know what to say."

"Yes, you do," Sophie added, looking into Elaine's eyes for the right answer.

"Maybe I do," Elaine admitted. "I think I'll see my son now."

Sophie smiled with pride. "I think that's a wonderful idea. I'll be back in a moment with Stevie."

Elaine stood by the stairs, waiting nervously. Her thoughts rampantly caused her to feel insecure. She reminded herself of all the years she imagined herself holding Stevie and now, in a matter of seconds, her dream would come full circle.

Stevie came dashing down the stairs and ran right toward the sweets that remained untouched on the tray.

Elaine stiffened. Her eyes welled up with tears. She felt as if her body was suspended in thin air. Her throat wouldn't allow even a breath to pass. She closed her eyes, almost ready to faint. She whispered to herself. "You're here. This is really happening. Let the past go. Let yourself love him. After all, he's your son."

Stevie walked over to Elaine. His eyes were focused on hers. Elaine was silent.

Stevie looked over toward Sophie and asked, "Hug? Stevie hug."

Sophie smiled approvingly.

Once again, Stevie looked up at Elaine. Then with slow, cautious moves, Stevie placed his arms around Elaine, squeezing her tightly.

In a slow, unsteady fashion, Elaine leaned down, meeting Stevie's arms and holding him. She looked into his eyes and kissed his forehead, whispering, "I do love you."

Chapter 26

While driving back to the hospital, Elaine actually found herself singing along with the radio. She couldn't remember the last time that happened, but she knew it was a long time ago. Life was getting better.

Each time Elaine stopped for a red light, she looked into the mirror and practiced what she would say to Martin when she got to the hospital. She would tell him what a fool she had been and how she should have trusted him to understand about her sister. He was the kindest man she had ever known and she didn't know why she was so foolish. Martin and Sophie were right. Stevie was kind and gentle. Just like his father. She had wasted so many precious moments and she was never going to allow herself to be fearful about the truth. Her whole life had been filled with secrets and pain, and that was over.

It was late when Elaine returned to the hospital, but she still sat beside Martin, waiting for him to get up so she could share her news. Elaine reached for Martin's hand and held onto it tightly. "You were right. We have a wonderful son. I wish you could have been with me. When I felt Stevie's hand in mine nothing else seemed to matter. It seemed so right, almost as if I had never been away.

"Martin, I love you and I hope you can forgive me for all the pain I've caused you. I'm going to try my best to make everything right. I promise you that your mother will know her grandson and, most importantly, Stevie will always be a part of a family — our family. If you'll have me."

It wasn't more than a couple of seconds before Martin finally opened his eyes. Elaine was so happy for the moment to explain everything. Just as she started to describe her day, Martin smiled at her. "Are you kidding? 'If I'll have you?'"

"You heard me?"

"Damn right I heard you. There is nothing in this world that would make me happier. You know how much I love you. We are a family. Elaine, you're going to be a great mother. Even if something should go wrong with the surgery, I know Stevie will have his mother at his side."

Elaine spoke with confidence. "You're right. We are a family. No doubt about that. And forget about something happening to you. You will be fine, and I am going to be there helping you every step of the way. Got that, Doctor?"

Martin smiled with a strong sense of relief. "Got it."

About the Author

Based in Chicago, Illinois, Marsha Casper Cook is an award-winning American author, scriptwriter, and writing coach who also provides audio books to her readers. From children's books to romance novels, her literary craft has touched various readers. Her books are a well-developed portrait of her target audi-ence whether they are kids, teens, or adults. Although Marsha was born and raised in Chicago, she explored other places to widen her knowledge on writing and human relationships.

www.ingramcontent.com/pod-product-compliance
Lightning Source LLC
Chambersburg PA
CBHW070457120726
47910CB00003B/1062